IMMORTAL ABERRATION

IMMORTAL ABERRATION

MY MORTAL MEMORIES I

CALUM LOTT

First published in 2025 by Virtue Publishing

The moral right of the author has been asserted.

Word count: 33,430

Cover artist: John Devlin

Cover typography: Rachel St Clair (Claymore Covers)

Interior cartography: Joshua Hoskins (Noctua Cartography)

ISBN: 978-1763518179 (Ebook)

ISBN: 978-1-7635181-6-2 (Paperback)

ISBN: 978-1-7635181-8-6 (Hardback)

THE NEXUS

ABHORRENT LUUG — A sapient species that once nearly wiped out the entire galaxy.

ASCENSION — The act of ascending into the higher dimension that is the Cos Realm.

BLACK HEART— Black spheres in the cosmos spawned by Malnetha, through which all its foul energy and influence pours into the waking world.

CAOS — A curse word derived from the Velutra's disdain for the influence of Chaos.

COSTHRALL — The energy responsible for all life in the cosmos.

COS REALM — A higher dimension within which resides Costhrall's pure energy, through which Velutrans ascend to travel the vast distances of the galaxy. The Great Ocean Above.

CRYLUSS — A transmutable element that generates immense energy.

CRYORB — A minute grenade.

CRYSTALA — A fluid transparent armour composed of countless minute organic machines. They can be detached from the user's body as one larger mist to form weapons, move things, or even for flight.

DREADMIND — A slur for those who've lost their minds to Malnetha. Slaves of the Zenlian Empire.

THE ELAN VITAL — The essence that gives Velutrans their sapience. When one dies, the elan vital is believed to return to the Cos Realm—back into Costhrall's endless energy.

GRAVITY SHEATH — An engine that can create moveable bubbles or sheaths of controlled gravity.

LUMENSHIELD — A moveable energy shield. Can be combined with other users to form larger and stronger shields. Once overpowered, the shield will break, putting it on a sixty-second cooldown.

MALTHEZUUL — The territory of the Zenlian Empire.

MALNETHA — The malevolent force responsible for helping create the cosmos by shaping Costhrall's energy. Also the name for a non-physical disease that causes corruption, madness, and decay.

MINDSCOURER — An ability to search one's mind by using a specialised crystala.

NEXUS — The supreme collection of information and data that resides within an artificial space.

NOPAINE SERUM — A serum that completely nullifies physical pain for a short time.

REBIRTH — The ability to be reborn after death. Highly forbidden and secretive tech in the Velutra.

SAGE — One of ten who lead the entire Velutra of Valsollas. Five humans, five illuavans.

SAGESWORN — The title given to those chosen to one day become a Sage.

SENYAR — The strongest known material in the Velutra.

STARFUSE WARHEAD — A weapon that harnesses the power of an exploding star.

VELUTRA OF VALSOLLAS —The largest and most powerful society in the Valsollas galaxy. Home to the humans, illuavans, coavlens, warlifs, sultaoss, and feyzarans.

VELUTRAN VIRTUES —The virtues that guide Velutran society. Prudence. Justice. Courage. Temperance. Love.

ZENLIAN — A race of Malnetha-infected beings.

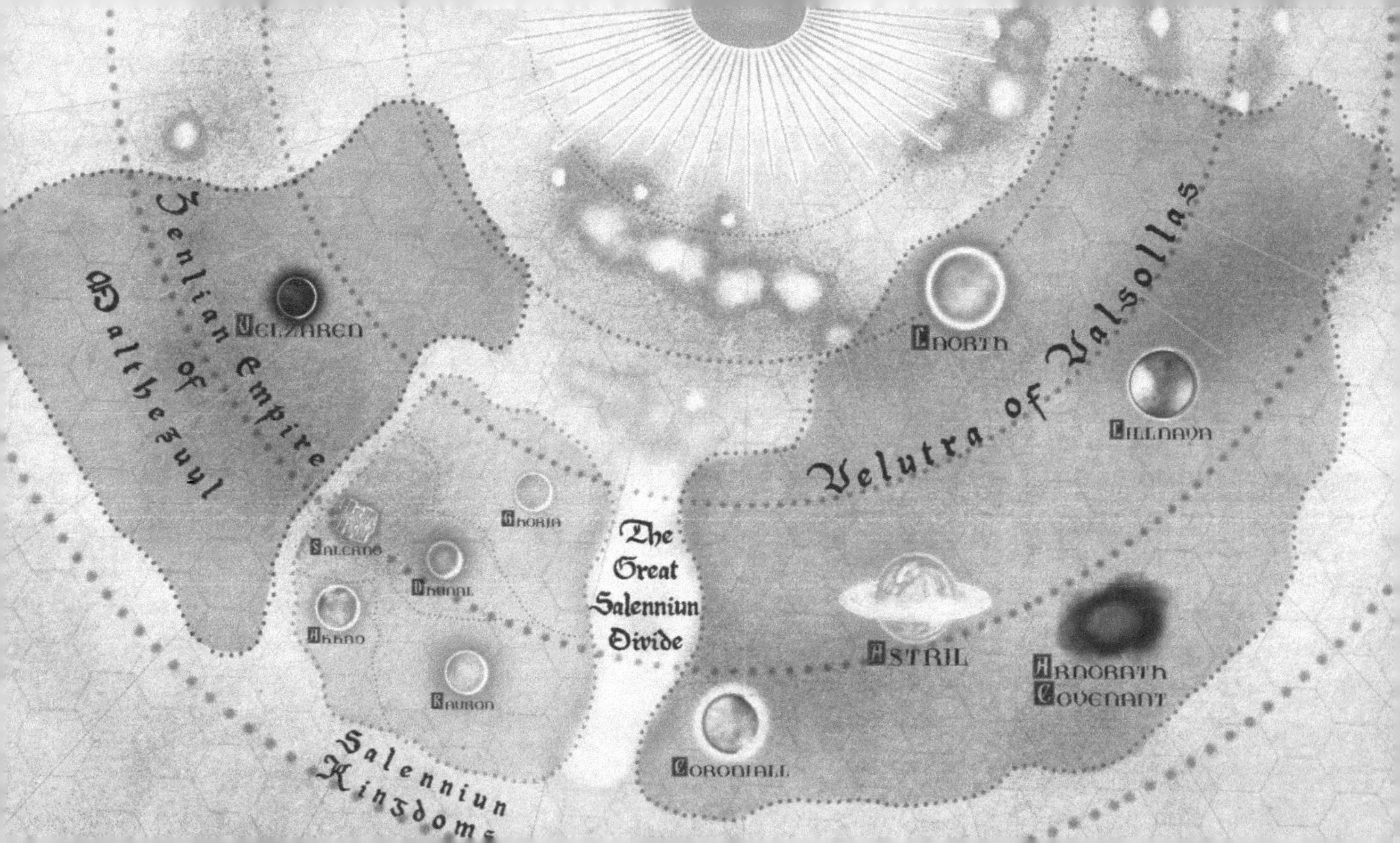

Zenlian Empire
of
Walthezuul
Uelzaren
Salenniun Kingdoms
Ghoria
Salerno
Unanal
Herro
Rauman
The Great Salenniun Divide
Velutra of Valsollas
Enorth
Lillnava
Astril
Hanorath Covenant
Coroniall

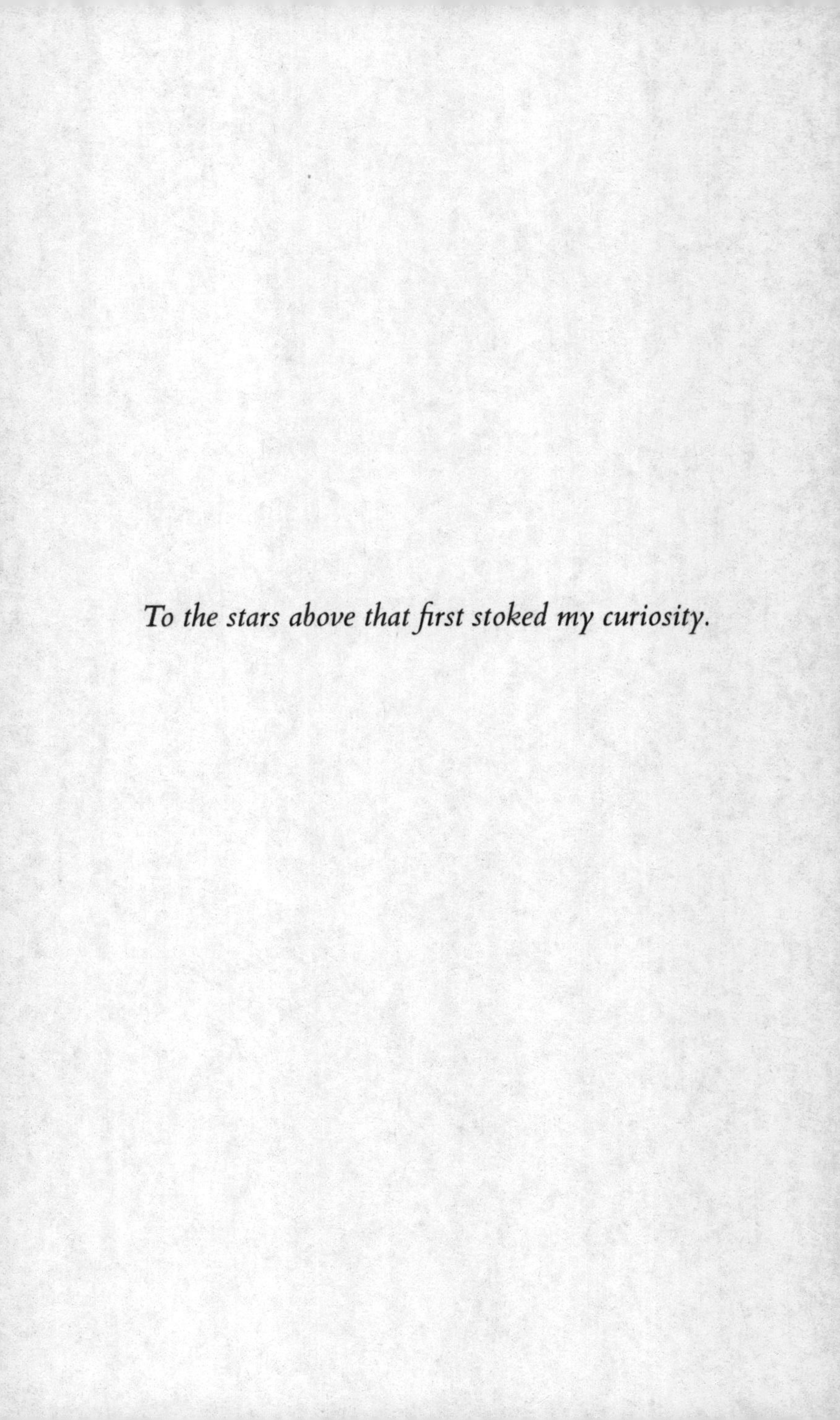

To the stars above that first stoked my curiosity.

CHAPTER ONE

A Nascent Dawn

I never intended to taste immortality.

Bastion found me yanking a knife out of a gurgling throat, my hands and face drenched in dark blue blood. I whirled around, snarling like a dreadmind as he stepped from the shadows, a pale green glint in his eyes. When he marked the corpses strewn about my feet in that festering alley, a thin smile of admiration cracked his lips.

I don't even remember why I was there. My best guess is that I'd stolen something I shouldn't have. I had killed before, but always out of self-preservation. Never greed. My childhood was a time of cold, hard survival. Later on I learned that's what Bastion saw as well, though to my scared little eyes, all alone in that bloody lane, he was just another enemy.

I lunged at him with my knife. He made no movements, except for his widening smile. Bastion was twice my height, so I struck right at his stomach, but my blade screeched against his crystala armour, translucent purple shimmering around him. I cursed as I was flung backwards in a whirl of disorientation, but before I could grasp what was even happening, Bastion's hand was clenching my throat. All the air, all my strength, squeezed out of me like I was nothing. Dangling there against that towering human, it felt like an eternity before Bastion dropped me with a wet thump onto the corpses I'd made.

"Here I was minding myself on this rank planet when I stumbled upon a meek little warrior. Oh, how causality flows."

I said nothing, but my eyes screamed hate.

Bastion scoffed. "Is this really the life you want to live, kid?" He paused, waiting for an answer, or another attack, but when neither happened, he knelt down and his harsh countenance softened. "I can guide you to a new life. One free from this miserable existence of scavenging for scraps and killing needlessly. The Black Ocean Guild can set you free."

I balked as Bastion lifted me from the cold, bloody ground and set me on my own two feet, but I settled as he continued speaking.

"You can travel the galaxy with us. Behold all its beauty and terrors. We will refine this uncouth rage of yours into a sharp sword as you fight alongside your new family."

Standing amidst a pile of corpses, it should have been obvious why Bastion chose me. If I was that proficient in killing at such a young age, then fully trained I'd be a fierce sword for the Guild.

He certainly wasn't wrong. Yet having no family, no friends, and no attachments also meant I was a perfect candidate.

"What's the price I must pay?" I asked. I was only a child, but years of stumbling through the decayed streets of Deladus had taught me that there was a cost to everything in life. Often a painful one.

Bastion smiled. "A life in the Guild will leave permanent scars, inside and out. You will watch those you come to love die. In the end you will most likely lay down your own life for the Guild, for the greater good. But in return, you will live a life of virtue, honour, and trust. You will find belonging. The decision is yours." He stood and turned to leave. "Meet me here tomorrow should you wish to accept."

The eyes of the dead stared up at me and my numb eyes stared back. When I pulled them away, all I remember seeing was the blood staining the pores in my small hands. I knew others would come for me once they found out what I'd done. I knew the chances of me surviving the night were pathetic. Desperate, broken, and naive—I accepted right then and there.

We left that very same day. I remember looking back on that planet, my homeworld, and thinking about all the suffering I'd endured just trying to survive. All those who'd betrayed me, all the violence I'd inflicted and had inflicted upon me. Every sleepless night, every desperate day. All I had ever known was mired within that little sphere, that murky speck drowned in darkness absolute.

Still to this day, Deladus is a crime-riddled nest of scum and desperation where those who can't face their own realities addle their minds with vile compounds. Nothing more than just another forlorn world amongst countless in the vastness of Velutran society—a small sliver of our galaxy.

I've never been back to Deladus. I never want to. But I have to admit, even from out there it held a quiet beauty I could not deny. It made all my grievances seem so pathetic, and in that moment, I knew I was ready for a new beginning.

I'd left the planet and risen to the void on several occasions, but I'd never gone far into the dark reaches—I certainly hadn't ascended to the Cos Realm. I'd heard stories about that higher dimension ever since I could remember, but they seemed just that—stories. Though I didn't really believe in anything back then.

"You will feel your mind and body dissolve away," Bastion said, right before our vessel ascended. "We will hurtle across the galaxy as we become one with everything that ever has and ever will exist. The ocean of life will soothe all your past, all your sorrows, for you are merely one sundered part of it. It will fill you with vigour and confidence. There is nothing to fear, Ludaan. Are you ready to take the plunge?"

Everyone remembers their first time ascending, and I am no different.

The journey was exactly like Bastion described, at least upon reflection. It was a transcendent experience of hallucinations, healing, and self-discovery. Even now

I struggle to put it into words. All I know is that visceral memory of my first ascension still fills me with hope today.

After I descended back to the waking world, that boundless warmth and vigour lingered in my limbs for some time, but no matter how badly I tried to hold onto that feeling, it eventually faded, just like everything. The restless dread that Deladus had developed within me crept back in as I floundered amongst an unfamiliar world full of strangers.

From birth, I'd never had what many in the Velutra would call a normal childhood. I had no fond memories of playing pretend, no veil formed around me from parents to block out the harsh truth of the world. I suppose I was lost like all children are, yet I had no one to lean on. Nothing but my senyar-sharp instincts.

That all changed when the Black Ocean Guild took me into their fold and I accepted them as the family I never had. Bastion and my new kin thrust me headfirst into the art of warfare and trained me relentlessly for decades. They lifted me up, only to knock me back down, hardening my bones, my mind. Although I revelled in every second, it took everything I had not to quit. To survive.

We were always on the move and never settled long enough to call a place home. Fortunately, our home was with each other. In that first year alone, the comforting hull of the travelling vessel we called the Mother Guild carried us across the galaxy to a dozen different worlds.

I experienced different beliefs, used technologies beyond my wildest imagination, and consumed exquisite foods. I killed my first dreadmind. I'll forever carry that moment. I saw blazing stars up close. I watched several die in great flashes. We even skirted the edge of a black heart that was in the middle of devouring a star, dragging everything into its lightless depths.

I knew early on that this was the life I was supposed to live.

From the very beginning, Bastion told me that the Guild's secretive purpose was to keep forbidden tech just that—forbidden. But it was only when I'd truly earned my place nearly a decade later that the truth was finally revealed.

I stood in the golden hall of graduation alongside Rier and Leonyd, two of my closest friends who I'd shed blood, tears, and laughs with. Leonyd had spared me a devious wink of pride, while Rier remained solemnly stoic—just like always. I dwelt somewhere between the two, though I can still feel the excitement stirring in my chest, the pride lifting my vital. We all knew from that day forward we'd be cleared for actual missions, though little did we know what truly laid ahead tomorrow, nor over the next century of unyielding warfare.

But back then, right as Bastion slipped the golden signet ring on my finger, the knowledge of Rebirth flooded my mind like a river of starlight. I heard Rier and Leonyd mutter something in disbelief, but all I could do was stare dumbly back at Bastion, like the naive fool I was.

Reborn after death. What a godly power—a violation of all things natural in the universe.

Needless to say, the Guild did whatever was necessary to keep Rebirth out of civilian minds. That's perhaps the strangest thing by far: no one else in the Velutra knows it exists.

I struggled to fathom the impact if that knowledge escaped our frail grasp. All those fragile minds suddenly awakened to the cure of all their fears, for without death we have no fear and with that great loss, we lose all sense of morals, of common understanding. The clamouring and murdering, the betraying and lusting would ravage the galaxy with devastating cruelty.

At least that's what I thought for a long time, but that day changed everything.

CHAPTER TWO

Scourer of the Mind

"What have you found, Carellus?"

The Mind Scourer was a thin woman, her pale flesh covered in golden runes of ritual. Most of her body was draped in black seamless robes and she moved as one with the dark chamber.

"Vileness," she hissed, then she smiled, golden vertical lines glinting on each of her perfected teeth. "Though I have glimpsed something that may be of particular interest to the Guild. Something coveting."

I focused on the Zenlian corpse suspended before me. I'd seen a thousand before, made a thousand myself. It was otherwise unordinary. A naked human with sickly white skin, so much so that it seemed to glow. His right arm had been augmented into a long gun, and carved upon his bony chest in old blood he bore the symbol of Empress Zenli, Her cursed self.

I said nothing, but gave Carellus' emerald eyes a hard look, urging her to spill what she had found and to not waste my time.

A fiendish grin blossomed on her face as she whispered, "A Rebirth Doc."

My whole body tensed. We knew little about Rebirth technology save for its illusive ability to reanimate a life into any vessel, anywhere after death. Our task was not to understand it, but to destroy it and the Docs themselves who conducted the vile practice.

"He's imprisoned in a Zenlian fortress," Carellus added.

I frowned. "Imprisoned?" Rebirth Docs were elusive enough, but in all my long years I'd never heard of one being captured.

Carellus stalked around the dead body as though it were her trapped prey. The head of the Zenlian corpse was shrouded in a black mist, from which a single tendril swayed down to the frayed ends of golden hair at her neck, connecting their minds as one.

"He's being held for Empress Zenli. She's coming to claim him."

"Why? What importance is he to her?"

She grinned. "Is that not your opus to deduce, brother?"

I stared down her taunt. Though we weren't genetically related, everyone in the Guild was bonded as family, whether we liked it or not.

"Do not test my patience," I growled.

Carellus narrowed her glowing green eyes back on the corpse. "None of their minds were kind enough to reveal, though one can imagine why Zenli has uses for this Doc's tech."

I scoffed. "She's already immortal."

"And is Her intention not to be the only one? Yet why then keep the Doc alive?"

"Is that not your opus to deduce, sister?" I replied, mirroring her snark and thin smile.

I shuffled my stance around, my boots stirring the layer of black dust that covered the floor, and the pungent remnants of Carellus' connections to the dead wafted up. She was always busy.

"What else have you found?"

"Schematics," she answered, stretching her long bejewelled fingers. "Of the fortress where the Doc is being held."

I scanned the shadows of the chamber. The walls were lined with more suspended Zenlian corpses. "Have any of the others confirmed this?" Before I absorbed all the information and took it to the Guild Mother, I needed to ensure it was legitimate.

Three other corpses jerked forward from the shadows to a sudden stop, suspended either side of the first. One had two swords for arms, but no head—not our doing. Another had no augmented weapons and its mouth was twisted open in a frozen scream, black tongue lolling out. The last one had dead eyes embedded all over their rotting flesh, staring back at me. I'd seen it all before.

"These three also possess broken fragments of the same knowledge," Carellus said. "It seems that they were ordered away to Nuaster to bolster the forces there; alas, they failed under the sharpness of your cleansing blade. The schematics I pieced together of this fortress also came from a dozen other corpses, though they knew nothing of the Rebirth Doc."

I tapped my teeth together, deep in thought. "Ordered by who?"

"The Nameless Lord, they call him," she answered, a raspy chuckle in her throat. "They may have lost their minds to Malnetha, but they have not lost their sense of irony."

In their worship of Malnetha, the Zenlians murder, and so they grow in power and influence over the other mad slaves until one claims themselves as lord over some foul dominion, only for them to die laughing as I cut them down. Yet like a pestilent weed, they always grow back. It is a never-ending cycle, despite all we do.

"What did they know of this Nameless Lord?"

"Very little," Carellus said, hushed. "They were never in his presence, but always commanded by one of his servants." She sniffed and her countenance tasted revulsion. "I can still smell the fear he instilled into their blackened minds."

The knowledge of the Rebirth Doc drove me on, and as I turned to leave, I spoke to Carellus through thought. *"If Zenli is coming to claim the Rebirth Doc, then we must hasten a plan. Send everything you've gathered. I go to the Guild Mother."*

"Yes, brother," she replied.

"Oh and Carellus?" I added. *"Prepare yourself. If we're to move on this fortress, I have a feeling you'll be accompanying us."*

I heard her salivating laughter as I stepped out of the room. *"Fresh minds to scour are a boon for us all, brother."*

CHAPTER THREE

The Mother Guild

The command bridge of the Mother Guild was where I felt the safest in the entire galaxy.

As I stepped inside the vast domed chamber, I was met with grand arched windows rising side by side, out through which the endless void glittered with stars. Our fleet of greatswords were anchored before the planet, Vaccemon, a vast green sphere of bitterly gaseous wastelands where we had just wiped out a hive of Zenlians and thankfully never had to return.

Yet now I had an uneasy feeling we were about to leap into a darker abyss.

I strode forward, and a congregation of cospriests scurried out of my way, their long white hair swaying as they did so. I recall the way that some of them lowered their heads in respect, and I suppose fear as well. I sometimes wonder if fear was a creation of Malnetha or Costhrall, because despite its terrible nature, its true purpose is to keep us alive. I was a dreaded force for the Guild, a cosmic killing machine, and yet fear has saved me more times than I care to admit.

As I marched across the polished white floors, the sound of my feet muted against their sacred sheen, I could not help but think of the first time I was brought here by Bastion. As a youth, I marvelled at the resplendent statues of those who had come before me, peering down like golden guardians wielding their weapon of choice. They lined either side of a bridge that jutted out towards a raised circular platform at the very centre of the domed chamber, below which were three other sunken tiered levels filled with a rolling sea of pale green mist, from which wisps swayed like tendrils reaching into our waking world from the Great Ocean Above. It always reminded me of a Cos temple with its elegant grandiosity, and the gentle hum of crystalline waterfalls. It was serenity teetering on the edge of chaos.

The Guild Mother and Bastion were already waiting for me on the platform, both hardly unchanged since the day I was first brought there over a century ago. They were stoic like the surrounding figures carved in stone, though their living eyes narrowed with grave concern as I approached.

When I came to a stop, my hands went behind my back and I gave a soft bow. "Guild Mother. You've absorbed the intel Carellus has discovered?"

"We all have," she answered, voice calm and regal as ever. The Guild Mother's tight uniform gleaned scarlet traced with gold, matching her penetrating crimson eyes and lush hair held aloft by aureate jewels.

Appearing on the end of her words, a perfect projection of Sage Tienza coalesced between the others. He was adorned in ethereal robes as though the cosmos itself had folded around him; planets, stars, and galaxies, all drifting around the great black.

"My Sage," I said, my reverence bowing deeper than before.

The Guild mother had summoned Sage Tienza to counsel us on how to proceed, the same wisdom that led the entire Velutra. Tienza was greater than any fighter in the Guild, myself included, but he was also a master diplomat and philosopher, trained in countless facets of Velutran life. My respect for the Sages was as strong as my devotion to Costhrall itself.

And yet it was Tienza's sole responsibility to shoulder the burden of going against the Virtues and hiding the existence of the Guild from the other ten Sages. He always handled that moral blight nobly in my eyes. We were a secretive sect for a reason, and had every intention of keeping it that way.

"Let us proceed," Tienza said, ignoring my courtesy. I'd been in his presence enough times to immediately sense a perturbed change in his tone, and by the look Bastion gave me as well, so did he. "Costhrall has provided us with a rare opportunity, but we must act swift. Zenli has been our bane for too long. It is time we end Her once and for all. We must capture this Rebirth Doc alive and scour the secrets on how to do so."

"The Guild has not tread that dark path for a reason," Bastion objected, always keeping his composed expression. "If we are to learn their secrets then we may become just like them."

"That's why we birthed the Dead Mind," the Sage replied. "And why each of you subject your memories to its cleansing touch after every mission. The virtues of the Guild will always remain uncorrupted, but it is time we adapt." He gave Bastion a hard stare, then looked straight across to the Guild Mother. "If Empress Zenli covets this one Doc, then they must be of great importance to Her. Perhaps he is Her personal assistant to immortality and has gone rogue."

After I left Carellus, I had spent my journey to the command bridge thinking about why Empress Zenli would want this Rebirth Doc so badly. As far as we knew, Zenli had lived for almost seven hundred years and showed no signs of relinquishing Her cursed life. The most logical idea I could come up with was one the Sage had also suggested.

I glanced at the Guild Mother, and in her majestic, yet prolonged quiet, I sensed her considering the idea to capture the Doc alive.

The Sage added one final point of persuasion. "If not for understanding Rebirth, we must find out what other secrets their mind holds. We fight a perpetually losing battle. We must learn how to permanently kill these undying zealots. We must learn how to kill Her."

"No," Bastion protested, far sterner this time, wrath stirring at the edge of his lips. "We should just obliterate the entire moon and every wretch with it."

"Your input is always valued, Bastion," Tienza replied, composed and lordly. "Yet this is not your decision to make. What say you, Guild Mother? Are you aligned with me? Do you want change? Do you want to rid this vile tech once and for all? Do you want to cast Zenli into the black heart from whence She came? Then we need to capture this Doc alive. We need to be swift."

"And what if this is a trap?" I queried in the absence of her answer. I was only present because I was Bastion's second and would be taking over his position in the coming years, but the Guild Mother always bid me freedom to speak my mind, even in the presence of a Sage.

Tienza finally graced me with his imposing gaze. "Do you doubt the Mind Scourer's ability or the validity of the Zenlians'?"

"They know how we operate," I answered, somewhat diminished. I always struggled to look the Sage in his eyes, but considering the gravity of the situation, I made sure to hold them firm. "It would not be the first time they've baited us with information like this."

"Ludaan speaks truths," Bastion agreed to my relief. "This bears all the makings of a trap."

I knew Bastion didn't want to lose any more Guilders under his watch. He'd grown weary from the losses those last few years. I did not blame his reservations then, especially not after everything that happened.

In another brief silence, the cospriests who I had stormed through began a low chanting. It was accompanied by an ambient noise that reverberated within the grand chamber as though the sound itself emanated from every particle in the air, right at the edges of my ears.

The Guild Mother finally spoke up, caution in her voice. "Sage Tienza is right. We must adapt. Leads on Rebirth Docs are far too rare to not take a chance on. If there truly is one imprisoned in that fortress, then we will capture them—alive."

She was not wrong about such leads being rare, and not letting things slip through our grasp was what we were trained for. Back then I wasn't as weary as Bastion. My edges were still as sharp as ever and all I wanted to do was what I had trained a lifetime for. Purge Zenlians.

The entire dome suddenly dimmed its lights, the polished white stone now brooding dark shades. Right before me and those gathered, a projected map of the Velutra appeared, thin blue lines marking its borders and inner territories.

The map then enhanced outside of Velutran territory—somewhere we travelled far too often for my liking—focusing on a pulsating black star. The view enhanced further until we looked upon a dark fortress clawing its way up from a dead grey moon.

"It's Velutran made," I said, pointing out the style of the architecture, the great spires, the ramparts and overall defensive layout. Zenlians were not capable of such creation, only corruption. "Though it has long since been defiled. Why do we know nothing about it?"

"The Great Erasure was three centuries ago," Sage Tienza answered. "It must have been lost then along with much of our precious history."

"*Bastion,*" the Guild Mother said with a sudden urgency in our minds. We were running out of time and when it came to the specifics of mission planning, it was customary to forsake the respect of spoken words and allow thoughts to flow much quicker between our minds. "*I know your thoughts and that you already have a plan to assault this fortress. Spill it.*"

Despite his demur, Bastion remained poised as he followed his orders. "*Based on the scoured schematics, the Rebirth Doc is held up in the lowest dungeons in the very heart of the hollowed-out moon.*"

While his thoughts drifted into my mind, the projection of the fortress changed to match his words, displaying the hollowed-out core of the moon and a labyrinth of tunnels, running all the way to the surface and inside the castle itself.

"*The only way we're going to be able to catch them by surprise is if we descend proximity close,*" Bastion continued, simulating the arrival of our fleet. "*The chances of our own destruction are minimal, but not zero. If we ascend immediately, we can arrive just shy of three days; that gives us thirty minutes to prepare while in ascension.*"

"*And if Zenli is already there?*" the Guild Mother asked.

"*The whisperings of Her coming only started right before we purged those who carried this intel, though I imagine there was a delay from the one who leaked the message. Nonetheless, if She's travelling all the way from Malthezuul then we may just get there beforehand.*"

"And what if She shows up while our forces are already inside?"

"Then we fight until the bitter end, Guild Mother."

Bastion may have been against the plan to begin with, but once decided on, he did his opus like a true Guilder.

"The Mother Guild and her sisters shall deal with the swarms and whatever other surprises they throw at us on the drop. Every company will split into swords of sixteen. Some will assault the upper levels of the fortress as a distraction where they may face this Nameless Lord, while my swords will lead the charge to the dungeons." At that moment a hulking form of rigid silver with two immense cannons crashed onto the moon's surface. *"A voidtank will puncture through this gate on the lowest exterior level. Three other companies will rally to our gate and we'll proceed inside."*

"Will four be enough?" I interjected. Although we'd assaulted fortresses like this one plenty of times, I'd also been entombed in the merciless hordes of Zenlian chimeras enough to permit my doubts.

"We want it to be small enough to avoid every cursed minion coming to swarm us," Bastion answered. *"Their focus must be on repelling our larger offensive in the upper fortress. However, we'll have other companies forming checkpoints along the way so we may call upon reinforcements."*

I voiced my concerns like Bastion always taught me. *"But we have to assume that the Nameless Lord will immediately know we're after the Rebirth Doc and act accordingly. What's going to stop them from killing the Doc upon our arrival?"*

"*We can only trust that Zenli wants to keep him alive at all costs. It has been so thus far.*"

I nodded. "*We must also consider that the Nameless Lord might not be in the spires like the intel states, but down in the dungeons with the Doc and all his spawns wreathed about him.*"

"*I understand your concerns, brother, but that is what we are trained for.*" Bastion called me brother, but he was the first father figure I ever had. "*We will act accordingly and deal with whatever comes our way. It is the Guild Mother's command.*"

"*And we shall see it done,*" I said, proudly.

"*If the scoured knowledge is true,*" Bastion continued, "*then this Nameless Lord took up residence six years ago and put his enslaved dreadminds into renewing its fortifications. It is said to be a fairly weak force inside, not yet fully ripe, but that is one thing I will not wholly believe. Nonetheless, the dreadminds and chimeras nested in there will scatter from our attack. We will break them.*"

The projection shifted to a vertical tunnel which ran all the way to the heart of the moon. "*Once we reach here, we fall down this long shaft. After that, there's another network of tunnels until we get to the main shaft where we'll hack the grav-sheath and it'll carry us down to the dungeons. From there we will be blind as to where the Rebirth Doc is exactly being held, but by then Carellus should have scoured a more precise location.*"

"*And your plan for getting out of there alive?*" Sage Tienza asked. I had no doubt the military prowess of his mind held an answer, but he also knew that Bastion was the one who would be leading the swords into battle, the one who would be spilling his own blood.

"Once the other companies break through their respective gates, I'll have them secure waypoints to keep the exit free." As he spoke, Bastion rolled his neck. He always did that when he was anxious. *"When we have the Doc, they'll collapse on us and we'll punch out the way we came in. Yet if previous assaults have taught us anything, it's that we cannot count on such a plan. The Zenlian labyrinth runs deep. We may find alternative escape routes to the surface, at which point we will hail for collection."*

After a hefty pause, the Guild Mother finished aloud. "So be it. The capture of this Rebirth Doc is our primary objective. Second to that is the death of this Nameless Lord." Cleansing as many dreadminds from the galaxy as we could was our third, I thought. "Finalise the battle plans and prepare the Guild. Send the hail, Bastion. We ascend immediately."

"This will be a new dawn for the Guild," Sage Tienza said. Then he bestowed us with the Velutran adage when heading into peril. "May the Virtues guide you all in my stead."

The Guild Mother, Bastion, and myself repeated the customary answer in unison with a soft bow. "Costhrall protects us."

The projection of the Sage disappeared and after a nod from Bastion I turned to leave.

Marching out, I stared up at the tall arched windows in the back half of the dome. They were full of different shaped and coloured fragments all puzzled together to tell stories of the Guild's past and heroic deeds. I could not help but picture myself amongst the splendour of their glory, yet they'd all died to earn their place up there and so I cast the thought away, miring myself in the present moment.

In the end, my life didn't matter. I was merely a sword for the Guild to wield as they saw fit, and wield it fiercely they did.

CHAPTER FOUR

Descension

"Descension imminent."

Bastion's voice rumbled in my mind as I opened my eyes. Outside the transport, the universe passed by in gushing rivers of pale green, upon which drifted emotions in fleeting visions of my life.

You'd think that after so many years of travelling through the Cos Realm that it would become mundane, but no. While it was true that I'd grown accustomed to the hallucinatory effects, we still only skirted the lapping tide of the endless Ocean Above.

Some of the company had been seated, some were lying asleep as though it were just another mission, even though they knew it wasn't, but that's how we were trained. Why we were the best. I trusted every single one of my company with my life and theirs with mine—it didn't matter that some weren't human like me.

I'd been standing the entire time, relentlessly going over the battle plan and fortress schematics, as well as running simulations for all that could go wrong. Bastion may have been the commander of every sword in the Guild, but I was still responsible for my own company, and I'd do everything in my power to make sure they made it out alive.

I put aside the plans and looked ahead at the stirring soldiers. They were all shuffling from the sides into the centre of the transport like a mindless hive until they found their formation in four rows of four. From my position at the rear of the cabin, Leonyd—the company's second in command—stepped over from the side and punched me in the arm, his fist a dull clang against my armour.

"What's that brooding scowl for?" he teased, a smirk twisting on his broad face. "You're not losing your edge, are you, Ludaan?"

"It's nothing," I lied, glancing away. Whereas on previous missions I would have been eager for battle and quelled my doubts by now, there was something brooding in the pit of my stomach, gnawing away at my confidence.

Leonyd shook his head. He knew me better than that and he hated it when I became distant. "Why do those who truly know and love us bother trying to deceive us? We can see through them like cryglass and yet they deny their own truth and push others away." He placed a firm hand on my shoulder. "Is it to protect themselves or protect others? Either way, it is foolish, and beyond you."

"Your ability to see through to my elan vital is an inconvenient virtue, brother." Then I came clean, making sure to look him in his eyes, though I did not want anyone else to hear. Fear's greatest weapon is company. *"I cannot place it. It's almost as if Malnetha is clouding my mind."*

"Fear not," Leonyd replied. *"You are shielded by your brothers, bathed in the guiding light of Costhrall. Focus on the edge of your sword and rid it from your mind. This is who we are, Ludaan. Bane of the cowering Zenlians."*

All I could manage was, *"Cos protects us, brother."*

Leonyd smiled. His face blushed with dark violet as a mist rose from his crystala armour around his head, coalescing into a mask of a growling creature with horns and thin violet eyes that stared back. He spun around, returning to formation, though the back of his helm showed an equally tormented monster.

I summoned my own helm and my crystala vibrated around my head, its countless organic-machines settling against my skin until it felt as though nothing was there. Enhancing my vision and surroundings, it allowed me to look back on myself and my mask of contorted bird-like features adorned with short golden wings on either side.

Every fully fledged sword in the Guild wore horrific monstrosities as our battle attire to stoke fear into the eyes of our enemies and keep us as the faceless servants we were. Mine was taken from a flying creature I killed after it tore a nice hole in my stomach. I suppose remorse is why I chose to wear it as a mask for all those years.

I felt a ping in my mind from Bastion. He stood at the front of the cabin, maskless, but crowned with slick grey hair. Despite two hundred and forty years of living—nearly one-hundred years my senior—his appearance and vitality had hardly changed since he was forty.

"You are the Guild's sword!" Bastion shouted in thought to every company. *"The chosen few who can deliver the Velutra from tyranny and corruption. We will capture this Rebirth Doc from the wretched Zenlians and finally put an end to this vile practice."*

"For the Guild!" everyone cheered.

In my mind, I repeated a mantra I'd collected over the years to still my mounting disquiet. *I've faced death countless times. I'll face death countless more. My crystala is my sword and shield. Costhrall flows through my elan vital granting me strength. Costhrall lends me its light to blind the darkness. I've faced death countless times. I'll face death count—*

A door hissed opened behind me, pulling me from my mantra.

Two cospriets stepped in. Adorned in their emerald robes, they held silver swaying balls that breathed out hazy green trails as they walked amongst our ranks, blessing our imminent descension with a sickly sweet scent and a murmuring chant.

I normally didn't care for their ritualistic benedictions, they were just that: rituals with no proven results. My belief in Costhrall was on a much higher level than that. However, with this mission's risky proximity-close descension, I admit I was glad for their presence.

As the cospriests stepped past me, I formed my sword, the violet mist gleaming with my crystala's power. I tightened my grip on the hilt and cut the air, a soft, susurrating sound like shards of raining cryglass reverberating around me. Perfect for carving mindless Zenlians.

Leonyd spoke up. "Carellus will have a field day picking the Rebirth Doc's mind."

"Or perhaps she will finally lose hers," Rier muttered beside him.

I said nothing but as I was making sure everyone was in formation, I marked Carellus standing with her eyes closed to my left in the shadowed corner. Black trailing mists twirled around her fidgeting hands as she muttered invocations, echoing the chanting cospriests.

"Hey, Leonyd," Suchine shouted in front of me and to the right. "Don't forget you owe me all that nomismo if there's a Doc down there."

Rier scoffed. "Are you making wagers with him again, Leo?"

"He's losing them," Suchine corrected.

"Don't get too ahead of yourself," Leonyd called out in that obnoxiously bold, yet comforting voice of his. There could be a thousand dreadminds surrounding us and his voice would always make me feel immortal. "The Plague could be waiting for you down there."

The same day I learned about Rebirth was the same day the older Guilders tried to haunt us with stories of the Plague. He had become an almost mythical figure who had plagued the Guild since its inception millennia ago. A shadow lurking amongst the endless voids. No one alive had ever interacted with him before—if he was even a man as the stories told—but the accounts were enough to put the fear into even us—warriors hardened by Zenlian blood.

Now Leonyd was bent on doing the same to the younger generation. I used to hate that about him, though the sound of laughter that spread throughout the cabin still brings joy to my mind. Memories of a better time. If only I could have seen that in the moment. Instead, I stayed grimly silent, the mention of the Plague only adding to my rising agitation.

"Why are you always risking that name, Leo?" Rier groaned, the disapproval in her voice emanating from a black mask that was an open jaw with sharp teeth. "One could swear you want to bring misfortune upon us."

Leonyd bellowed a laugh. "Quit your superstitious fretting. The last time I didn't say that wraith's name, everything went wrong." He swung his massive rifle around and up onto his shoulder. "It'd be misfortunate if I didn't mention it."

"One minute until descension!" Bastion called out.

The cospriests exited the cabin and the transport's engines quietly hummed in preparation. Besides that, and the faint trickling of our crystalas, there was a distinct quiet that loomed all around us, as though the Cos Realm itself kept the air hushed with its gentle breath.

I pushed the creeping thoughts of the Plague away, and sent harsh words privately to Suchine. *"You don't want to be right. You shouldn't ever want to face a Rebirth*

Doc, I thought I already carved that into your skull?" A part of my blade broke off like a trail of mist and smacked his helm with a screech. *"Cos forbid, Zenli Her cursed self shows up. Then nothing else will matter. We'll all die the same: screaming while they laugh, drunk on madness and our flesh."*

Suchine had only been on a handful of real missions and I needed to put fear into his mind so he would stay sharp. So he would remember what we were up against.

"Get it together," I yelled out, addressing the entire company. "All of you! The Guild Mother has tasked us with the capture of a Rebirth Doc. We will achieve our mission. We will vanquish any spawn of Malnetha that challenges us. We are the Guild's Sword!" I thrust my gleaming blade high and all the others raised their fists and gave a cry.

"Thirty seconds!"

Suchine turned around to look at me, his black beard exposed beneath his helm, the face of which was imitating a corpse woken from death. I'd found him not looking much different, face beaten bloody into a pulp—that's why he chose that mask. When I healed him, I gave him the same offer Bastion gave me as a child. I've made many poor choices in my life, but bringing him into the Guild wasn't one of them.

"I won't let you down, Ludaan," he said.

"I know."

"Ten seconds!" Bastion shouted. *"Clusters have descended around the target. We will be swifter than the darkness at the edge of the universe. For the Guild!"*

"For the Velutra!" everyone cheered.

I closed my eyes and my crystala muted all sound. A moment of quiet always calmed me before I let the chaos in.

CHAPTER FIVE

The Velutra's Sword

When our transport dragged itself down from the Cos Realm to the waking world, the line my mind drew between the two was briefly blurred, vague, and I fell out of consciousness. Upon returning to my body, I took a deep breath to ground myself back in reality, and then peered outside.

Consuming my view was the cold white sheen of a vast icy ring, wreathed around a planet like a twirling dancer. Aqua storm clouds ravaged the world in perpetual mindless rage, yet from a distance, the smooth swirls of blues and greens were terribly serene.

The transport locked onto the target and enhanced my view. Floating between a narrow channel of the gas giant's ring was a small moon, a pale marble amongst many others. The countless beads of ice surrounding it were like white strokes of a painter's brush and were warped in undulating waves from the moon's gravity.

A barrage of vessels, including my own, shot down to the moon, leaving pale green descension rivers in our wake. We'd risked our own destruction descending so close to a physical object, but it was one we were all willing to take.

As the moon swelled in my field of view, I let sound back in through my crystala, just in time for a cacophony of violent screeches to rattle my ears.

My mind snapped back to inside the transport, watching over all the Guilders still standing strong in their ranks. The shields outside were already under heavy fire from the fortress' cannons and the few defending voidcrafts, but they held for the moment, keeping us steady. I gripped my hilt tight, grinding my teeth in anticipation. Battle was calling.

Then the shield shattered with a distorted crack.

I hardly had the time to register it before another blast collided with the hull and, despite my crystala armour, the impact knocked the air out of my lungs. The lights in the transport went dark, and all I saw was a violet haze and spinning stars where the front of our vessel had been obliterated.

Dread twisted in my gut at the thought of losing Bastion, but when I regained my senses, he was still standing there against trails of leaking purple. His crystala kept him safe from the cold nothingness that surged inside and bolted him to the floor as our transport spiralled out of control.

"We're not dead yet!" Bastion called out. *"Get ready for the drop!"*

I tensed, drowning in the sound of my rapid breaths. Fear coursed through my veins, but somehow throughout the chaos I felt that some of it was due to the close connection I had to Suchine's mind, his dread leaking into my own.

"*Don't hesitate once you're out!*" I cried. "*Let the grav-sheath—*"

"*Dropping!*" Rier shouted.

The floor vanished beneath my feet and the grav-sheath cast me out. I plunged through the emptiness of the void like a human meteor, everything around me a blurry storm. Flares of light burned in the corners of my eyes, shrapnel of ruined transports screaming against my crystala.

Amidst all that mayhem, I trusted in the grav-sheath. Adrenaline pumping, I closed my eyes, waiting for it to safely release me on the moon, while my mind drifted to the moment Bastion found me. It always managed to provide some comfort.

The semi-transparent grav-sheath silently slammed into the moon's surface, and as it broke apart, safely releasing me, I exhaled with relief. Then my instincts took over and my crystala vision pierced through the arcs of rising dust, scanning my surroundings. Eight other swords had landed nearby and their violet glows were already rallying towards my location.

"*So much for our original plan,*" Leonyd remarked, the first to arrive.

"*Perhaps you would have cared to stay on the transport,*" Rier replied, arriving a second later.

"*Shields up,*" I ordered.

Suchine and the others gathered nearby and a translucent violet sphere folded around us. I added my own to strengthen it and assessed the situation. Only then did I realise that we'd lost two Guilders in my company during the drop, the loss of their lights in my mind piercing me with a stark coldness. But I could not dwell on their deaths there; that would have only got more killed. I repeated their names and pushed their dead faces out of my mind.

"*Ascrin and Sath are gone,*" Suchine muttered in shock.

"*How the caos did they break our shields so easily?*" Leonyd asked.

"*Better yet, how the caos did they scatter our sheaths?*" Rier put in. "*I placed everyone on this marker, yet the others landed all over.*"

On the edge of the group, Carellus produced a coveting smile. "*The Rebirth Doc must truly be here.*" She wore no sharp plates of armour like the rest of us, and was unchanged from before with her tattered black robes and golden symbols painted over her body, but her transparent crystala protected her with the same strength as our own. "*These are no meagre Zenlians.*"

"*Do not act so surprised,*" Cosrick mocked. He may have been the most devout in the company, but that didn't stop Malnetha from twisting his mind. "*You know our enemy. They always find a way to counter us.*"

Leonyd postured. "*They wanted us to come here.*"

"*Enough!*" I snapped. I located Bastion and the rest of our company several kilometres away, but he spoke to me before I did.

"*The mission is still a go. Converge at this rally point, then we move on to the fortress.*"

"You heard him!" I shouted, punching Suchine in the arm to get his mind out of shock. *"Move!"*

And like that, we were off, our crystalas propelling us at an unnaturally fast speed through the moon's light gravity. We punched out of the cloud of dust we'd made from landing and the battlefield became clear.

All around us lay a terrain of blasted craters and dead grey hills, though we knew from the schematics that the Zenlians had tunnels everywhere underneath the moon's surface. As we flew over the first lightless pit, Rier cast down a swarm of drones and their violet glow was quickly lost in the darkness as they searched the depths.

Straight ahead, I focused on our target. Despite our distance, the Zenlian fortress loomed above us like a jagged mountain. It was a conglomeration of misshapen spires and thick battlements, all black as the void, faint distortions rippling all over as its shields absorbed a cosmic barrage. Cannons, each thrice as large as our own transport, protruded from the castle itself like arms of a giant machine vomiting a constant torrent of black and crimson beams up at the Guild fleet.

A storm of transports were still barrelling down to the moon, some involuntarily, others already in wrecked pieces. As our group raced forward, we were alerted to one's trajectory, and right before it crashed into the surface, we darted out of the way, rainbow flames licking at my crystala before they were extinguished by the cold, crushing void.

Still racing forward, I peered up at the raging battle. Larger than the moon itself, the Mother Guild was shaped into a vast greatsword, slicing through the universe. It made for an easy yet hard to bring down target. Around it, and amidst a storm of flaring flashes, were other greatsword-shaped crafts, though far lesser in size, as well as a host of even smaller droned warring vessels, all buzzing about as they waged war from above.

At that moment, on the edge of the Guild's fleet, I witnessed black spears tearing into existence, their lightless tips piercing the stars. Then they collapsed, and large mangled voidcrafts filed out into the intensifying mayhem, wailing upon the Guild's fleet.

"Let them taste Cos' bite!" Cosrick cried.

All that mattered was that they held them off until we completed our mission. Even I found myself thinking prayers to Cos that Zenli didn't show up before then. Alone, as we often were, we could not have fought off Her ruinous armada. But the Guild's resources were only a star in the galaxy compared to the true might of the Velutra—secrecy certainly had its weaknesses.

As we ascended a rolling grey hill, Bastion and the rest of the company joined us, but we did not stop moving or talk. We locked onto our target and raced down into another broken gulley, yet the dead surface was always inclining upwards to the fortress.

It was then that I noticed a small craggy mountain off to the right that was not there in the scoured intelligence and I shuddered to think about everything else that was going to be wrong.

"The scouts were just destroyed!" Rier cried. *"Chimeras! Thousands of them!"*

"Plenty of Zenlian pets to crush," Leonyd said, eager as always.

"Guild Mother," Bastion called out. *"How much longer until you take the fortress' shields down? Or do I have to come up there and do it myself?"*

I fought back a bleak smile. Bastion was as good a leader as they come.

The tip of the Mother Guild was oriented to directly face the castle, and running through the centre of that greatsword gleamed a ruinous dark purple as it answered Bastion's call. In a great flash, a pillar of light shot down like a starry arrow and it smote the top of the fortress, overpowering its main shield in a shattering blast.

"The Velutra's sword!" Cosrick yelled in victory, holding up his own sword.

We all cheered as we raced onwards, but we hadn't got much further when all over the moon's grey surface, more holes started appearing, the edges continually crumbling inwards as the blackness grew. Although our crystalas kept us suspended off the ground, the reverberations of the groaning moon sent shivers through my bones.

"They're coming up!" Rier shouted.

"My rifle is hungry," Leonyd muttered.

"Don't stop!" Bastion ordered. *"We need to get to the gate!"*

Out of the growing pits, small insect-shaped crafts propelled straight out and up to join the void battle, already spewing a shower of hate. From those same lightless holes, pale creatures began crawling out. Endless hordes of them.

Perfect, I thought, gripping my hilt tight. *Here we go.*

Chapter Six

Send Death

"Guild Mother, send death!" Bastion commanded.

The perfect voice of the Guild Mother responded in our minds. *"Impact in two seconds."*

Through my crystala's vision, a faint blue cloud covered the closest scurrying horde, and I knew to stay clear of the incoming blast's radius. When I next took a breath, a great flash blinded the universe and the entire moon trembled. If there was an atmosphere then the shockwave might have slowed my crystala's momentum, but the moon was stripped clean, leaving only the eerily calm silence of the void.

My helm automatically dimmed the blinding light and I soared over the sunken crater that the blast had created and through the pillared trajectories of dust, blood, and guts splaying up and out. I scanned the growing haze for any chimeras still alive and then, manipulating barrels onto the flat of my sword with my mind, fired deadly fragments from my crystala at anything that moved, blasting holes through their skeletal bodies.

I led the company at the front while Bastion guarded the rear. As we neared the fortress, great spheres of white light erupted all across the landscape as the Guild fleet showered the moon with starfuse warheads, obliterating hundreds of chimeras with each devastating explosion.

Yet straight ahead and sprinting directly towards us on a relatively flat plain was another horde. They all scurried on their four bony legs, long blue antennae-like things attached to their heads flowing behind, while faceless dagger-filled mouths chomped in anticipation.

"Cleave a path through!" I cried, putting the tip of my sword forward.

Flying closer to the ground, I punctured through anything in my way, but before long I had a dozen chimera corpses piled in front of me and so I swung my blade to the side, flinging their butchered bodies out into the low gravity. I continued to slash and fire at anything I could, severing several heads and limbs with a single swing, while those behind me finished off the scraps and hacked at the flanks.

"Grind them into the moon's dust!" Leonyd rallied.

No one in the Guild—myself included—had been genetically spliced to become physically superior. Using such forbidden tech would have violated our entire purpose, though many of us still carried the genetic strengths from the Splicing Age millennia ago. What we had was our naturally hardened bodies, tempered by gravity, by the cold void, by the discipline of our relentless training and our superior tech. Not to mention our sanity.

Once we broke through the mass of white bodies, we continued up the sloping grey hillside. The outer wall of the castle quickly engulfed our entire view, its ragged construction deformed, its blackened dominating presence casting no reflections.

Eventually we came to the fortress gate. It rose out of the lifeless moon two-hundred metres high, its front covered in frozen blue serpents, their fangs puncturing skulls. Protruding higher above were cannons like serpent mouths firing blast after blast, their power shaking the ground. I'd seen plenty of horrors in my time, but I shuddered to think what I'd find inside on this occasion.

We were the first company to arrive and so on our approach I had our soldiers form a perimeter and merge our shields into one transparent violet sphere.

"Our tank was destroyed in the drop!" Bastion relayed. *"Drills, break this caosing gate down!"*

Four Guilders darted to the centre and misty trails peeled off their crystalas until the mass coalesced into a massive spinning drill. Silent in the vacuum of the void, it slowly devoured a tunnel through the hardened gate. Bastion moved up beside them, the hot white sparks enhancing his already commanding presence.

The thrill of battle pounded my heart as I peered out at the barren terrain, across which flowed floods of white chimeras while the dazzling light of our warheads burned with cosmic glory.

I glimpsed Suchine a few soldiers down the line, and although he held his dual axes firm, I knew he was trembling inside. I couldn't blame him. Even I could not rid the knot of worry eating at my chest.

With nothing to do but wait and watch, I repeated my mantra. *I've faced death countless times. I'll face death countless more. My crystala is my sword and shield. Costhrall—*

I marked movement from two other approaching companies from either side of the castle walls. When they arrived, they fortified our perimeter and joint shield, just in time for my crystala to ping with more movement, but this time from above. I whirled around to see holes cracking open in the castle's walls.

"Above!" I yelled, directing everyone's attention to the chimeras crawling out. These ones were made of pure black bones, engraved on which were mad scribbled Zenlian runes. Instead of dangling antennae like the others, pistols had been augmented onto their eyeless heads which fired a hail of dark blasts down upon us.

"Costhrall shields us, you blasted things!" Cosrick bellowed right next to me, banging his sword against his large shield. He had a bad habit of laughing in battle as though the same madness that infected the Zenlians had taken him.

Fusing my blade solely into a rifle, I unleashed a constant trail of blitzing fire up at the descending horde, the recoil redirected and suppressed so well that all I felt in my hands was a dull vibration.

The creatures exploded and splattered, their corpses flung back into the fortress and beyond, along with trails of their pale blood—only their viscid feet had kept them fixed to the stronghold. But their numbers were so dense that our combined fire could not wholly repel them and they crashed against our barrier.

"Hurry up and get through this gate!" Bastion pressured the drill wielders.

"It's senyar!" they replied, blaming the strongest known material in the galaxy. *"We're going as fast as we can!"*

"I don't care what it is. Break it down!"

I fired a cryorb from my rifle that ripped through a swarm of the chimeras with bolts of white lightning, but they kept on coming, our shield gradually shrinking inwards. More chimeras completely surrounded us on the ground, their snapping jaws gnawing on our barrier. I spun around, spraying death, piles of carrion quickly rising.

"Send danger close fire," I requested to the Guild Mother. *"Shield integrity at sixty percent."*

"Brace for impact."

I stepped back to the centre of our barrier, right behind the drill, and the others followed. The strikes came down in front of us like a pelting rain of pillars, the drumming impacts stirring up more dust and sending heavy vibrations through my crystala, rattling my feet. Every wretched spawn caught in its path was obliterated. Even the ground itself was pounded down under the might of the Mother Guild's cannons, but so too did our bulwark lose nearly all its strength.

Heedless of their gaping wounds and doom, the swarm of writhing bodies not targeted by the cannons above continued to press down on our shields. There we stood our ground, firing everything we had as a descending tide of blood and guts suffocated us.

Then the drill cracked through the last of the gate and crystala drones poured inside, relaying a cavern overrun with chimeras.

"Starfuses!" Bastion called out. *"Ludaan, forward. Leonyd, get these blasted things off us."*

I stopped firing at the horde right amidst our ranks and with a flick of my mind, my rifle disintegrated back into my crystala. Then I pulled a radiant five-pointed star off my back and darted forward to the drill. An opening formed in the back, and I quickly jammed the star inside.

Every company carried five starfuse warheads—spread amongst the senior command—but only for use at the utmost need. However, with this mission, time was of the essence and so we were more lenient in their use.

The drill pulsed and ejected the warhead through the hole in the gate into the fortress. I darted out of the way, as did the drill wielders and anyone in the line of sight. A second later, a white pillar of light shot out of the fortress, piercing the enveloping dust cloud and trailing to a point of nothing.

At the same time, the warhead Leonyd had tossed up and outside our shield erupted, consuming everything with a blinding luminescence, shattering the rest of our shield in consequence.

The moon below my feet trembled from the blasts, but before the stunning light had receded, I'd already put my blade forward as I rushed inside.

CHAPTER SEVEN

Storming the Keep

As soon as I put my foot inside, a cold presence pierced my heart.

I'd never felt such a thing before. It was like the blazing green eyes of a baleful god were fixated on me, unblinking. It stopped me dead in my tracks, made it hard to breathe. I hadn't been back in the waking world for long, so I wasn't sure if I was still hallucinating or if it truly was some kind of malicious entity that dwelt within.

"*What the caos was that?*" Leonyd shouted as he came in right behind me.

"*You felt that too?*" I replied.

"*Fiery eyes watching,*" was all he said.

That omnipresent gaze vanished and I snapped back to the present. Shaking my head out of the stupor, I pushed forward, Leonyd right behind me. We didn't get far before a hail of fire crashed into us. The blasts chipped away some of my crystala, but it was nothing it couldn't handle. Nonetheless, I instinctively took cover behind the closest pillar to minimise its loss, crunching cracks of stone ricocheting around me.

The manipulated gravity well was precisely confined to the castle's perimeter and so with an atmosphere restored—albeit a stagnant concoction of rotting air and corpses—sounds returned to my ears, though I would have rather remained in the silent and airless hostility of the void.

"A slumbering dread has been awoken," Carellus whispered as she came inside.

I gave her no response, though her words stirred my unease.

All the other Guilders funnelled inside after us, and while I warned them of that watching phantasm, they were all just as rattled as it perceived them, but there was no time to unpack it.

The rest of the companies formed a line between a row of jagged columns on the edge of a larger chamber. Leonyd and I had cast violet flares ahead, illuminating the hollow that at first glance appeared like a deep cave lined with sharp rocks, naturally worn by the decay of time, yet upon closer inspection, there were pathways amidst the cragged mounds of stone, an unnatural order about it. All along the high walls, Zenlians peeked out of tunnels, flashes of red firing down at us.

Out from the cover of our pillars, I aimed my sword-rifle up and let it sing. I managed to hit a few and their bodies were ripped apart back into the tunnel or they fell down into the cavern with a wet splat, only for more to scurry through the muck of their fallen comrades to the edge and resume firing.

In between my bursts of fire, I pulled back behind the pillar and noticed a thick layer of white ash all over the floors from where the starfuse had obliterated the chimeras. The warheads we carried were different to the ones the greatswords used outside to pelt the hordes and other enemy crafts. Ours were specifically programmed to target organics—if it had been an indiscriminate warhead then it would have demolished the fortress gate as well as all of us.

Leonyd brought me back to the battle again. He was on my left, his massive rifle howling with his voice, "For the Guild!"

I spun around, my sights locked onto a Zenlian peeking out of a tunnel high above when it ceased fire and unleashed a shrill scream. Then all the others stopped and they retreated into the black tunnels, their laughter lingering in echoes. I shot the thing just in time anyway, blasting its leg off, but its head fell out of sight before I could finish it.

A disquiet fell upon the cavern.

The stala-feeders came in through the gate last, engulfing the room in their dark purple glow. The four of them wore silver masks that sparkled with grains of starlight, and besides their black armour that was no different to the rest of ours, large containers were strapped to their backs.

Bastion stepped forward from the line into the hangar. *"Send out the scouts!"*

The stala-feeders each called forth a mass of tiny flying knives and propelled them ahead into the cavern and many side tunnels.

"*What could that phantasm be?*" I asked Bastion, thoughts still in disarray. "*Why have none of the other companies already inside not reported this?*"

"*Because they have not experienced it,*" he answered.

"*Why?*"

"*I cannot say.*"

That uncertainty from the most experienced warrior I knew sent a dagger of dread down my spine.

"*The schematics are already wrong,*" Rier said, joining me, Suchine, and several others as we regrouped. "*This should be a voidcraft hangar. What do you make of this, Carellus?*"

The Mind Scourer stood behind the pillars, smiling, hands always fidgeting. "*I saw what I saw.*"

"*These lairs are always changing,*" I said, not intentionally defending Carellus, but trying to comfort myself and the others.

"*What of the phantasm?*" Leonyd asked. "*Has there truly been no indication of such a thing?*"

"*Nothing,*" Carellus answered.

Leonyd muttered a curse beside me. "*Remind me to wait until you offer good news instead of wasting thought. But the way the dreadminds fled like that, and the phantasm's gaze… I'm not one to run from a fight, but I…*" He trailed off and turned his horned helm away.

"*The dreadminds may have been called to defend their master,*" I said, answering his doubts, wondering if that presence was this Nameless Lord. *"As to the phantasm—whatever it may be—we cannot let it seep fear into our minds. Trust in Costhrall's light."* Then I turned to Bastion for guidance. *"Do we proceed?"*

I remember the way his figure solemnly peered out into the purple haze of the cavern, as though he knew what awaited him. His silver mask covered his entire face in circling lines, except for his left eye, which was uncovered and gleamed a faint green back to me.

"What would you do?" he questioned without the noise of the others.

On the last few missions he had frequently asked for my opinion on matters. I knew he was testing me as his years as a sword were coming to an end, but this was one decision I was not ready to make.

"Trust in your judgement."

"And when I am no longer here to guide you?"

"Trust in your memory," I said.

"And what would I do?"

"You would go on," I answered. *"Always forward. Always endure."*

"You must trust your own judgement," Bastion said. *"Trust the willingness of the Guilders who would lay down their lives for you. You must embrace the trust of Costhrall's light."*

I nodded along, though said nothing more. His resolve emboldened mine.

Two other companies arrived where we'd broken through the gate, though they remained there to secure the area.

Bastion ordered us on. *"Spear formation! Ludaan, move us out!"*

I shot out first, leading the tip of the spear on the ground, then the rest folded in on an angle behind me, gliding above the uneven mounds of stone, weapons scanning for threats throughout the cavernous hollow.

My legs felt heavier than before, my armour exposed, but the stala-feeders glided alongside us in the centre of the formation. Flowing from their silver packs were a host of misty tentacles, endowing our crystalas with re-plenishment, renewed strength flourishing around me.

Towards the end of this chamber, I noticed the jagged black stones that curved up either side of me had unnaturally grown into tormented faces and beastly creatures. The narrow path was made of flattened skulls and further out was littered with remnants of chimera and dreadmind limbs that squelched under my feet. I could not help a sliver of empathy for those who had been so mangled from the warhead, instead of being withered to ash like the rest.

I stopped as I passed two Zenlian bodies lying atop each other, limbs blown off but their heads still intact. I beckoned the Mind Scourer. *"Carellus, see what you can find before we move any further. Quickly."*

She glided above the ranks of soldiers, her exposed feet dangling in the air. She landed beside me, kneeling in a rank puddle, and then two black misty tendrils drifted off her robes to wrap around the Zenlian heads. Closing her eyes, she craned her neck as the connection opened and her mind was flooded with whatever was left of their cursed memories.

There was never a moment in her unsettling presence when I didn't think back to the early days of my training. I can still feel her hands like cold serpents slithering through my bones and my mind, acidic poison leaking from her sharp fangs, sizzling all my precious memories away into twisted nightmares. It was important we hardened not only our bodies but our minds as well.

Even now, I cannot shake the belief that there is something inherently wrong about rifling through someone's mind, whether dead or alive, sane or mad. Yet it had become a necessary tool in the endless conquest against the Zenlians, for without it we would have been left blind in the dark, blind from Costhrall's guiding light.

After a moment, Carellus murmured. *"Zorthan Illesar. That is our Nameless Lord."*

I knew the Zenlian tongue well and that zorthan translated to the word *hollowed*. While illessar had no translation, my mind pinged with a correlation from the nexus.

"Sagesworn Illessar," I breathed out. "She went missing six years ago."

I'd never met her, such was the Guild's secrecy, but I always paid attention to those who were coming up in the ranks and would one day lead the Velutra alongside the other Sages.

"The same time when our Nameless Lord took up ownership of this fortress," Carellus added. *"Neither of these*

wretches have seen her, though they always felt her command-
ing presence.”

“*So this Sagesworn has fallen and become a Zenlian
Lord?*” Suchine wondered.

“*They will die the same,*” I assured him.

“*How causality flows,*” Cosrick said. “*We have been
brought here for a reason.*”

I suppose he was right after all.

“*What of our path forward?*” Bastion asked. “*Were we
deceived by the others you scoured?*”

Carellus took a second to answer, then she opened her
eyes, stood, and the black scouring mists reabsorbed into
her robes. “*I’ve updated several passages that were different.*”

“*And the Rebirth Doc?*”

“*They heard whispers of a prisoner,*” she said, nodding
with a smile. “*As far as they knew, he’s still down there.
That’s all. Procure me some more minds, preferably alive, and
I’ll see what else I can uncover.*”

“*Then we keep moving,*” Bastion said. “*Ludaan, onwards!*”

I spun around and continued on until I reached the
massive crag of this cavern that came down to the floor,
the wall of damp minerals shimmering with different
shades of black. With my blade burning against the
darkness like a dying star, I strode forward into the large
tunnel before us, the three companies falling in behind
me.

The passage shortly turned left and the jagged rocks
were polished away into a grand corridor of smooth
dark-green stone. The Zenlians layered their corruption

atop, decorating the walls with bones but also glaring, bloody runes that my helm dimmed. Their kind thrived in the pitch black, and although these runes cast light, they were sigils that strengthened their connection to Malnetha.

I slowed down as we approached a swarm of squeaking vermin the scouts had detected. Each was no bigger than my foot, but they packed the passageway, scurrying all over the floors, walls, and even the ceiling. I thought about gliding through the centre of them as the drones had done, but I did not trust the bioluminescent blue blisters growing out of their black fur and so I called up two stala-feeders. "Clear a path! Burn them back!"

Side by side the two Guilders marched forward and summoned a trail of mist from their packs over to their hands, which then ignited in torrents of crackling violet fire. They incinerated the squealing pests, pushing the rest backwards. Painfully slowly, I walked behind them, but we never stopped advancing.

"*We're losing too much time, brother,*" Rier said, close to my side.

"*Stay focused, sister,*" I replied, suppressing my shared concerns. "*You leave the worrying to me.*"

When we reached a junction, the scorched vermin scurried to the side passageways, leaving our route ahead finally clear. I picked up my speed, following Carellus' updated navigation route that sloped downwards deeper below the moon's surface level, but we didn't get far until my mind was alerted that the droned scouts sent ahead had been destroyed by a delirium of lurking dreadminds.

That did not stop us.

We sent another group of scouts ahead as I led the three companies onwards, my hands eagerly awaiting the thrill of battle. Yet that was still a minute away and as I raced through the empty corridors, my mind could not help but wander to the larger aspects of the battle and so I tapped into the feed of the main assault.

The Guild had punctured through the fortress in a dozen other locations, chiefly around the ring of inter-connected spires where we believed the Nameless Lord, this Zorthan Illesar, sat on her throne, though I still had my reservations, believing that she would be in the dungeons alongside the Rebirth Doc.

The battle status reported that we'd suffered heavy casualties on the initial drop from their shield-breaking weapons, though I already knew that. But now, every company engaged in melee were losing soldiers with every second we didn't complete our mission.

"All companies take heed," the Guild Mother said. *"Reported encounters with enemies wielding acidic projectiles that break shields. Extreme caution."*

"The same projectiles the cannons were spewing out," Rier assumed as we kept moving. *"Did you keep this information from us, Carellus?"*

"No," she replied. *"These Zenlians I scoured were not privy to such tech. Do not forget their hierarchy of knowledge. And do not accuse me of heresy again."*

The ambush that we willingly marched into didn't seem so appealing if some of them bore those weapons, but one of the stala-feeders who had sent the scouts ahead somewhat calmed my fears.

"The delirium ahead does not appear to possess such weapons."

"Then we save our remaining starfuses," I said. *"We still have a ways to go yet."*

"Kill them the good old way," Leonyd said. *"Shall we have another contest? First to crush one-hundred dreadmind skulls is the victor."*

"This does not feel like a contest-having day, brother." But in the end I was born to kill dreadminds and that's what I did.

CHAPTER EIGHT

Into the Black Heart

I punctured through the front line of Zenlians, my blade cleaving through several at a time, my tongue tasting murder. Swords carved, guns screamed, shields shattered, bones crunched. I was glad to see the edge of my company was still sharp, just as I had relentlessly trained them.

"Behold your fate, vile spawn!" Leonyd yelled, savagely sticking his rifle through a dreadmind's chest and blasting out the other side. "You are merely a vessel of reflection for what awaits all your cursed kindred."

We were a raging sea of violet against the oppressive shadows. The chamber itself was strangled in dead tree-like pillars, their cracked roots spreading all over like dead veins after sucking all the life out of its host. Pale green liquids dripped through the rocky walls and formed bubbling, bilious pools for me to kick enemies into, dissolving in seconds.

Amidst the foray, I saw the flash of Suchine as he plunged one of his axes into the knee of a dreadmind twice his size. He left it there and the brute stumbled while he spun around its back and sliced its head off with his other axe. The corpse crashed to the ground and his weapon broke apart, reforming in his hand. He paused, standing above his vanquished foe.

"Your rot ends now."

Two dreadminds raced up behind him, but I raised my sword-rifle and blasted their heads off from a distance. Suchine turned away, leaping back into the melee, his dual axes splattering dreadminds one after the other in a shower of dark blood.

I felt knives scratching at my back, but they bounced off my crystala with a sharp screech. I spun before they could strike again, and punched one in the chest, caving his body inwards with a bone-shattering crunch, while my blade severed the other's head. I couldn't help but feel a surge of superiority, of immortality, but I extinguished it. I always did my best to never let it consume me.

I snapped around as a distorted roar exploded on the far side of the chamber. A section of the wall had been ripped open, showering us with fragments of stone as more flailing dreadminds stormed into the foray.

"Show them Costhrall's light!" Cosrick roared.

"*Regroup!*" I ordered. "*Form ranks!*"

I wanted to toss a starfuse at them, but we were too spread out and couldn't form a united shield to protect ourselves from the blast. So we were forced to continue the melee.

A few of the closest soldiers fired out their cryorbs and a tempest of cracking white bolts pulverised the first wave of dreadminds, tearing their bodies apart in a flurry of gore. As the Guilders formed a line to fend off the newcomers, my attention shifted above to the carved stone paths where the dreadminds were firing down upon us.

"Leo, get up there and punish them!"

He happily obliged.

More were coming straight at me on the ground level and so I dealt with them first. One of the defiled things had four extra groping hands, while on another, eyes bulged out of a gleaming silver body where no human eyes belonged. I cut through its arm, ripped it off with my free hand, and impaled the other dreadmind through the throat with his friend's arm, then I heaved my blade upwards, splitting the first one in half.

Every dreadmind was different in their vile disfigurements, yet they all died the same, with their shrill laughter gurgling in their throats, though I ripped three of those out during the ordeal.

Heedless of their inferiority, the throng of dreadminds hopelessly writhed against our ferocity, blindly throwing themselves upon our weapons. Soon there was a field of flayed corpses at my feet, hunks of their bloody remains clinging to my crystala.

"Purge the fiends!"

Someone was always sounding battle calls. Some may think us no less sane than the mad Zenlians we slew; perhaps we weren't in those moments.

I leapt up onto one of the high passages to aid Leonyd and spewed out a heavy wave of fire, chewing all the dreadminds caught in the way into bits. I spun backwards and pinned a scrawny one to the ground with my blade, then my feet crushed his head with a sickening crunch, rotten brain and skull fragments bursting out. I yanked my sword out and swung it up with a wet tearing of flesh as it sliced through another covered in blistering boils, trails of bright blue bioluminescence splaying all over the floor and already-made corpses, sizzling them with disintegration and proving my instincts about the vermin earlier right.

"Mad-diseased cowards," I spat.

A restless urge twitched my hands, that unquenchable primal lust for battle burning in my chest. Malnetha often toyed with the mind when killing was involved. It didn't matter if it was its own cursed subjects that were butchered or creations of Costhrall. Killing was killing and that malevolent cosmic force fed off that.

I would not be the honest man I believe I am if I didn't admit that there were days when that uncouth rage within me won. It stirred within, a pool of corrosive hate, slowly withering away my resolve, my devotion.

I finished the last enemy close to me by grabbing the top of its small skull and pumping three blasts in through its mouth, then I ripped its head off and tossed it away as the body fell to my feet with a weak thud. I steadied myself and took two deep breaths to slow my pounding chest, but there was no time for relief.

"*Incoming!*" Rier shouted, directing all our minds to movement.

Out from the corrosive pools sprang mutated creatures, their shells reflecting a glimmering green. They landed on tall, yet thin legs, then with abnormal swiftness, they scurried forward like half-formed beasts, thin tentacles flailing off their sides. They had no head, eyes, or mouth; instead, fleshy cylindrical holes were sunken inwards at either end of their elongated bodies from which they began vomiting blasts with a melody of vile regurgitations.

"There's four of them!" Suchine shrieked as one landed right in front of him.

Up from above I watched one of the shell hounds unleash a storm of green fire that missed the closest Guilders and instead struck a pair of nearby stala-feeders.

"They're after the stala-feeders! Protect them at all costs!"

But it was too late. The attack burned through their crystalas with no resistance, knocking them backwards as large swathes of their bodies dissolved from the acid. They writhed on the ground alongside the culled dreadminds in a terrible agony no serum could dull, quickly falling silent. The other hounds did the same and just like that, half of our stala-feeders were dead, reduced to searing puddles.

The hound closest to Suchine stopped its attack and the way it shuffled around, I knew he was next. I leapt off the pathway above and as I flew down, I poured a great deal of my crystala into my blade and plunged the tip into the back of the creature's carapace. My sword's bite was deep, but not deep enough as it ground against the thick shell, so I pumped a cryorb down my hilt and cast it out of the tip.

The impact reverberated up through my feet with a strong bang, trickles of white light flaring out from the edges of my embedded sword. I winced as a small fleck of acid spat out from the gash and scored my hand, immediately burning a thin hole straight through my palm, but my crystala quickly poured in to seal the blotchy hole of melted flesh and pump me with a nopaine serum.

The creature merely shook itself, showing no other signs of pain or stopping. Standing atop the thing, I yanked my blade out and yelled at Suchine, who stood frozen below. *"Move!"*

He heeded my command but not as I had intended. Snapping out of his fearful trance, he lunged backwards, avoiding its fire, but at the same time, he hurled his axes forward at the hound's tall legs. They screeched against its hardened armour, but did no damage, and so they flew back through the air until they landed in his hands.

"It's completely covered in this shell!" he cried. *"How do we kill it?"*

"We'll find a way."

I jumped off its back and on my way down, my feet kicked a dreadmind in the head, smashing him into the corpse-covered ground. I killed a few more around me with quick cuts and a few blasts, before dodging another shell hound. All around, the other Guilders were hacking and blasting up at the things as they trampled from place to place across the chamber with terrible speed, blasting in return.

When I reeled around, I glared up. Atop one of the shell hounds stood a malformed creature of bone and white fire, blazing wings like tendrils of starlight. It stamped its emaciated legs and directed its mount back at me. In answer, I propelled myself up off the ground and thrust my blade straight through the skeleton's rib cage, my face touching the cold flames licking at its hollow head.

The impact smacked it off the hound and we flew across the room until I pinned the creature against the wall above. Its sharp gaunt claws scratched at my back, as did its serpentine tail, but I quickly formed a small, sturdy knife in my free hand and cut off one of its arms, then I brought the tip up and severed one of the mangled horns growing out the side of its head. The skin-starved chimera snapped its bony mouth at my face, but I yanked out my blade and let the creature fall to the ground with a clacking of broken bones. I plummeted after it and jammed my sword in the centre of its skeletal head, firing a pulse for good measure. The crimson light suspended in its hollow eyes went black.

I exhaled, then whipped around, studying the shelled beasts for a desperate second, looking for something to exploit. *"Aim for the holes where they're firing from! That's their only weak spot!"*

I leapt back into the foray, dodging the headless hounds the best I could, but on two occasions I got hit in the arm and leg, and I grunted in pain. The seeping acid only made minor wounds, and as my crystala healed them, I kept firing up at the narrow target on the creatures, tearing chunks of their sodden flesh away.

Leonyd's rifle screamed from above. *"Someone jam a caosing starfuse in them!"*

Easier said than done. Chaos had us in its grips and the only openings were the ones it released its death acid from, but as the battle wore on, I saw dark splits forming in their green armour.

"Their shells are starting to crack!" Cosrick called out. *"Keep at them!"*

The shell hounds had no mind or love for their mad kindred. One of their thrashing tentacles grabbed a dreadmind and pumped their acid into its head until it melted away. Another trampled the lesser slaves, while some jumped in the air, folded their legs up, and came down, using the bottom of their shells to squish whatever had the misfortune of being below.

I came back to back with Rier as a delirium of dreadminds surrounded us and threw themselves at our blades. I swept low and cut off the legs of the first two, while the gun in my other hand riddled them with holes. We made quick work of the crowd, but when I was done, I looked across the chamber in panic.

"Suchine!"

He smashed his axe into the head of a dreadmind right as a shell hound leapt into the air and was already coming down to squish him. He had no time to move, but right before it was too late, Cosrick appeared with his massive shield held above his shoulders and he braced himself as the bottom of the shell hound collided. The impact bent him to his knees with a shout of pain, yet he still held the entire hound aloft with all his might.

To his credit, Suchine did not waste the gesture. He darted out beneath the shell and then threw one of his axes up into the hound's fleshy barrels, striking a deep blow, and the beast recoiled off to the side, freeing Cosrick's shield and allowing him to freely stand tall once more.

The shell hound rolled over and back onto its legs, then with bewildering speed, it scurried back to Cosrick. Towering above him, all of the sunken barrels which it had been firing from tore apart, forming one cavernous mouth, a malicious green leaking out.

Cosrick dropped his shield and raised his blade high, its edges erupting in a storm of defiant white fire. "I am Costhrall's swor—"

The shell hound puked a flood of bile straight down that engulfed Cosrick whole. Hopeless, I watched as he fell to the ground with the acid, reduced to a sizzling puddle in the blink of an eye. The warmth of his presence was extinguished from my mind, leaving behind a cruel silence. Another of my soldiers, my family, gone just like that.

I let the rage take me. Screaming, I raised my rifle and fired three cryorbs. The wretched thing swallowed them up with its new mouth right as they exploded, arcs of white lightning lashing outwards, stripping off chunks of its shell and gooey flesh. With its insides and life essence eviscerated, the hollow shell hound collapsed to the ground with a deep thump.

Scanning the chamber, I discerned that two of the other hounds had been felled, their cracked shells lying lifeless and leaking.

Now only one remained. Everyone turned their attention to it and our blanket of fire continued to shred its cracked carapace, chunks of acid spraying everywhere. It wasn't long until the thing reeled and a wailing squeal emanated from its butchered body as it collapsed and died, slinking back into one of the bubbling pools.

"Back to the void," I muttered.

I looked about as the rest of the Guilders finished the few shrieking dreadminds that had survived and not fled. Her feet stained black, Carellus was already slowly stepping through the dead, her mind scouring mists shooting down here and there to scavenge what was left.

Once the killing was done—four of those shelled horrors, and three-hundred and twenty-seven dreadminds all sent back to the void—I simply stood there dazed in exhausted horror, staring where Cosrick had died.

Movement from a dead Zenlian at my feet shocked me back to the present. One of his eyes twitched, the sickly cracked veins pulsing as it stared up at me. I went to plunge my blade into his chest again, but the eye closed shut, while the other dead one remained open.

Frozen, I shivered as a foreboding rush sunk into my mind, one noticeably different from the watching phantasm upon entering the fortress. I'd seen illusions before of Malnetha's making, but mayhem and doubts still twisted my thoughts. I was either being fed a vision from the phantasm, still hallucinating from the Cos Realm, becoming infected with Malnetha and slowly losing my mind, or something else was actually watching me through that eye.

No one else said they saw anything similar, but neither did I speak up. Either in fear of them suspecting my sanity, or pride in believing that Malnetha could never corrupt me, I do not know. I focused on the edge of my sword to ground myself just as Bastion had trained me.

"Gather yourselves!" Bastion bellowed. "Tend the wounded!"

Our collective minds pinged all the injured—and all the dead. Of the three companies, we'd just lost over half of our stala-feeders and one third of our swords, as well as four starfuse warheads dissolved along with their carriers.

While some secured the perimeter, I shook off my encounter and rushed to help those injured, pushing piles of dreadmind corpses out of the way.

I knelt before one whose back leant against a pillar. Lonus was his name. He still wore his armour, except for his helm which he'd removed, revealing his defeated eyes and mouth dribbling with blood. I scanned his crystala and body, glaring down at the melted holes in his chest, stomach, thighs, as well as his left leg, which had been completely dissolved away. I poured my own crystala into his wounds to stop the bleeding, but he managed to lift his arm and put his hand against my breastplate.

"No," he sputtered, terribly faint. Then he spoke in thought. *"Save it for yourselves. I feel my elan vital slipping. It's too far gone now. I go to Costhrall's embrace. Farewell, my kin."*

I closed his eyes when they fell still, then closed mine and said a prayer to Cos.

A surviving stala-feeder came up beside me, resurfacing my urgency. *"Do it,"* I said.

We had them consume the bodies of the dead, violet clouds rapidly devouring their flesh and bone until nothing was left. Then they stored the essence of the fallen for safekeeping until we returned to the Mother Guild and could give them a true Velutran farewell.

Once all the dead were collected, I gathered beside Bastion along with the wounded. "Shall we send you back, brothers?" I asked. "We can divert another company to come and collect you."

They all stood steadfast, looking straight at me, but only one of the wounded spoke. "No, we go on with you. Until the end."

Bastion nodded to the stala-feeders and they used the remainder of their reserves to replenish the crystalas of those that were weakest first, then the rest of us balanced out our armour between one another. We were all equal in battle. Equal in death.

"Carellus," Bastion snarled, a roughness to his voice I had never heard before. "Have you found anything that might stop my soldiers from dying?"

The Mind Scourer was still stalking through the reeking chamber of corpses, though she promptly answered, unaffected by his anger. *"This shield-piercing acid is a creation of this abode's new Lord, Zorthan Illessar. Her Sagesworn mind held deep knowledge of our tech; alas, Malnetha has corrupted it to good use. I'm no mutagenacyst. Even then, they could not develop a resistance so swiftly."*

"What else?"

"Several of them have confirmed that there is an escape tunnel," she said, and the new schematics came to our minds. *"A grav-sheath that runs from the dungeons all the way through the moon to the other side of the surface."*

Bastion and I exchanged suspicious glances. *"We stick to our original plan. We leave the way we came in."*

Carellus returned to us, seemingly finished, scrunching her face with dissatisfaction. *"There is nothing left for us here. I suggest we move—while we can."*

Bastion growled, then turned away from her. "Advance!"

I led the companies over the mounds of mangled corpses and out through a small arched exit. It opened up into a vast subterranean hollow, a flat ring around a black abyss. The stala-feeders released more scouts and they rushed past me, darting down into the pit, their light quickly vanishing from sight. I stepped up to the precipice, my boots overhanging the edge as I marked a staircase curling down into hidden depths.

I'd been inside a black heart before, heard the whispers of Malnetha itself scratching at my mind. There are few things I've experienced in my long life worse than that moment. Facing that primal, cosmic force, that which is responsible for all the madness and cruelty in the world almost broke me. But I endured it back then, and I was resolved to endure this mission.

To our right, three other companies spilled out of a tunnel into this main ringed area, their violet glow merging with ours. However, on the distant side of the chasm, a delirium of dreadminds flailed out of a passageway, voidblasts firing across at us. The new companies formed a shield wall perimeter and blasted back while the commanders came to a stop before Bastion.

"We've lost eleven swords so far," one of the company commanders reported over the high-pitch cracks ringing out against our shield. *"Seven of them were our stala-feeders."*

I moved over to Bastion, glowering. *"The Nameless Lord guides them."*

"This acid is tearing straight through us," another commander said, clutching at his stomach. *"How the void did they make such a thing?"*

"How are we supposed to combat it?" the third commander asked.

"We will not cower against their tricks," Bastion snapped. *"We will face whatever they throw at us with the strength of Costhrall. Always forward. Always endure. We cannot delay any longer. I need some of your swords to go on."*

"They are yours to command."

Bastion directed some of the soldiers to merge with ours, though only enough so that every company present was now equal in numbers, stala-feeders and starfuse wielders.

"*Keep the starfuses,*" the first commander said. "*You're going to need them more than us.*"

"No," Bastion replied. "*We are all equal in battle. Equal in death.*" Then he gave each of the company commanders an approving nod. "*You hold this position, no matter what.*"

One of them banged the hilt of his sword against his chest. "*Every wretch that comes our way shall flee in horror.*"

They darted away to the front of the shield wall, blasting back the dreadminds. Bastion and I stepped up to the edge of that black pit and over the warped cracks I muttered the old adage with a grim smile, "Out of the void and into the black heart."

Bastion turned to me, his silver mask splattered with black blood. "*Don't forget the Void Realm beyond those black prisons,*" he said. "*There's always a darker shade, Ludaan. But wherever we go, we carry the glaring light of Costhrall to blind all our enemies.*"

Bastion raised his lance high and it pulsed with a violet flare. "With me!" he cried and he leapt through the shield, off the edge and fell down into the engulfing dark.

I remember a muggy and foul stench rising up. I remember the pit of unease that churned in my stomach as I jumped off, following the man who had become my father. I repeated my mantra to shed the fear, but it was the fear that kept my edge sharp.

CHAPTER NINE

Discoveries

I fell into that devouring abyss for what felt like an eternity.

Seeping into the outer layer of my crystala was the intensifying putrid scent of death, accompanied by a thickening stagnant heat the closer we got to the moon's core. The walls of the jagged rift eventually enclosed around me and as I slowed my descent, my feet planted back on the ground with a dull thud, though the safety of footing provided me no comfort.

Peering up through the violet glow of our group, vertical walls like sheets of night entombed us. Carved out of the wall directly ahead was a vast face, its screaming mouth forming a tunnel. Crimson and black liquid gushed from its eyes, splashing into pools below that scattered into many thin streams.

Through the jaws of the statue I rushed forward, Leonyd following close behind. Our path weaved through several tunnels until it opened up into a hazy chamber, the many flickering candles reflecting off the polished red floors. I slowed, then came to a stop.

Directly ahead hung the naked corpse of a woman, though her insides had been completely hollowed out, leaving only a pale husk of shrivelled skin and deep black holes where eyes and a mouth should have been. An altar of sewn-together corpses formed an arch of memoriam around her.

I edged closer as the others filed in behind me, the scent of burnt blood heavy in the air. A glaring light caught my attention and I knelt down, brushing my gauntleted fingers over a rune carved into the smooth steps made out of fused bone. It read *Zorthan Illessar*. "So this was Sagesworn Illessar's fate."

I looked back up at the hollowed body as Suchine inspected it, but dared not touch it. "She's shed her skin like a serpent, leaving behind this empty shell. Her own cursed Rebirth."

Leonyd gave a perturbed grumble. "She will not have slithered far." His head swivelled around the room. "This place is precious to her."

I stood, glowering at Bastion. *"We cannot give her the proper death rites, but we should burn her body."*

"I fear the rage that may bring upon us," he responded.

I feared it too, but I would not continue until it was done. *"I would bear all the hate of Malnetha if it meant giving any of my swords a deserved farewell."*

"And so it must be done," Bastion said. *"Be quick. We have to keep moving."*

"Suchine, set her ablaze."

His head whipped around, and through our connected masks I saw dread on his face. *"Why me?"*

"*You're a grunt,*" Leonyd said. "*Don't question your orders. Just do it.*"

"*Now,*" I finished. It was important for him to take part. I'd already burned and absorbed my fair share of fallen comrades.

Suchine hesitantly stepped back as a violet mist shot up and ignited the hollow shell of the Sagesworn's pale, yet preserved, flesh in hissing orange flames.

"*We shall avenge our fallen Sagesworn and obliterate this moon whole once our mission is done,*" Bastion said. "*But now the Zenlians press back our assault. We're running out of time! Move out!*"

I gave the burning Sagesworn one last look. The fear within me hoped to avoid her corrupted new form wherever she lingered in the fortress, yet another part of me hoped to truly put her elan vital to rest, to take some strength away from Malnetha. Regardless, I prayed to Cos that I'd never end up like her.

We left the chamber, though by the time the last soldier passed the burning altar, the Sagesworn had been reduced to a heap of ash. I proceeded through the connected passageways, kicking down doors that blocked my path as I went. Each room we passed was littered with their own flavour of cruelty and horror. Experimented creatures—some sobbing, others silent in death—whirring apparatuses of vile technology, and more altars of worship.

But when I burst into a larger cavern containing vats, I was frustratingly forced to a halt once more. Scattered across the room atop the ground were many pots, each twice my height and width, and covered in glowing runes. Dangling above them from a network of spider-like arms were dozens of cages made from spike bones, clinging to which were the malnourished arms of naked and groaning hostages awaiting their sentence.

"Vat captives," Leonyd said, his empathetic disgust mirroring my own.

I looked up into the eyes of an old man sticking his head between the bone bars. I wondered what world he had been stolen from and how long he had been here. If he knew any of the women or children beside him.

"*Guild Mother,*" Bastion said. "*We've discovered a group of vat captives. I suggest one company holding the position above the shaft to come down and escort them out. Advise.*"

"*Affirmatave,*" she replied regally. "*We've found several other harvesting vats across the fortress, though they've all been emptied. Get those poor vitals out of there.*"

One of the company commanders holding the position above hailed us. "*We're on our way!*"

"Get them down!" Bastion shouted, enforcing the Guild Mother's orders. "Above all else, our loyalty is to the Velutra and those who call it home!"

I was glad we didn't have to bring them with us, especially when we still had a good distance to go until we reached the dungeons in the heart of the moon where the Rebirth Doc was being held. Dead weight always meant dead Guilders.

I shifted my posture and, pointing my blade up to the cages, echoed Bastion's commands to rally the hesitating soldiers. *"You heard him! Second company, get them down! Third company in the rear! First in front! Haste!"*

Instead of securing the chamber, Suchine paused beside me. He stared as the second company flew up and began cutting the cages open and bringing the hostages back to the ground.

They were kept clean of Malnetha's madness—the best their masters could manage—so their bodies were pure when they splashed into the corrosive vats and their organic matter disintegrated into the energy source that would eventually power their weapons. But many often lost their minds before it was their turn and so they were set free, reborn as dreadminds.

I knew Suchine had never seen Zenlian vat harvesters in reality before because I'd led every one of his few missions, so I took a moment with him while I could.

"All the simulations and absorbed memories in the world cannot prepare you for the real thing."

"I keep learning that," he said, voice soft under his dead mask. "Guess I'm a slower learner than you'd like."

"No you're not. Never put yourself down. Only weak minds do that." I glanced down at my gauntleted fist. "It never stops. That's why our training is relentless. We must always be prepared to face the unexpected." I placed a hand on his shoulder. "You are a sharp sword, Suchine. The Guild is fortunate to have your devotion, your strength. Now we're about to move out. You best get back in formation. I'm counting on you."

He nodded and darted away.

Bastion stood nearby, watching his soldiers bring the captives back down. As they did, Carellus greeted them, gluttonously searching their living minds. I walked over and Bastion turned to me. *"You're good with him."*

"I learned from the best," I answered, then fell quiet, thinking about the dead Zenlian eye that had marked me.

"What is it that bothers you?"

I scoffed, uncomfortably moving my legs. *"Besides this entire mission?"* I looked away. *"It's nothing."*

"You cannot fool me," he said. *"Unburden your restlessness before it eats away at the company."*

Clenching my fists, I turned back to him, though I still kept what I had seen to myself. *"The last time I felt this way was when we were ambushed on Astimar."* I paused, remembering how one of Empress Zenli's Void Lords toyed with us before wiping out twenty companies. *"Bastion, Malnetha itself may be here. Or…what if Leonyd spoke the truth? What if the Plague is the Rebirth Doc we seek? What if we really are walking straight into a trap?"*

"We knew it was a possibility," he answered. *"But none of that changes the Guild Mother's command. We are swords and we must cut where our master swings us. Focus on the moment. On keeping your soldiers alive."* He placed a firm hand on my shoulder. *"All we can do is continue our task and trust in our own ability. Trust in Costhrall's li—"*

A wailing scream cut the words from my mind. As I spun to the source, one of the hostages lunged forward, trying to attack a soldier with a makeshift bone knife, but was grasped by the throat and held high above all the other cowering hostages.

"His mind is lost," the soldier reported, and the data rushed to my brain of his test indicating he was infected with Malnetha.

"Subdue him for now," I responded. *"We can't kill him in front of the others. We need them to be cooperative. And test them before you release them!"* The minds of our soldiers were being muddled by Malnetha. That would have never happened otherwise. I'd trained them too well.

A violet cloud wrapped around the prisoner's head and his body went limp.

I turned back to Bastion, my countenance grim. "There is no light in a black heart."

All the other hostages were quickly tested and brought down from their cages to a huddled group on the ground. Only three others had completely fallen to Malnetha and were also subdued. Looking back over the hostages and Carellus, I asked, *"Have you scoured anything of use?"*

"Nothing yet," Carellus answered. *"Only their lives and how they wound up here. Their eyes have been living in the black for a long time."*

"The other company is almost here. Keep searching."

Bastion nodded me on and I strode forward past the freed hostages, gleaming sword in hand. I looked across at that same old man, but for a split second, one of his aged eyes was opened wider than the other, cracked veins pulsating, staring straight at me. As if caught, his heavy wrinkled eyelids fell back down to normal.

I almost stumbled but kept walking because of Leonyd and Rier right behind me. If I was beginning to lose a grip on my sanity, then I wasn't going to shout about it. I subtly used the maltectus embedded within my crystala to test myself for the infecting madness, but I found no relief when it reported I was well within accepted levels for being inside a Zenlian lair.

My feet marched on while my heart drummed twice as fast. I struggle to remember what I thought was happening. Everything became hazy, uncertain. Oppressed. One thing I knew though was if someone or something was tormenting me through those widening eyes then there was nothing to be done about it. If I'd spoken about it then fear amongst the company would only have worsened, as would their mistakes. All I could do was keep moving forward. Do what I was trained to.

By the time I reached the position and was ready to move out, the company from above rushed into the chamber to escort the hostages out. They gave them each a little of their crystala to cover their scarred and scrawny bodies in plain robes, as well as heal their wounds and help them glide back up the shaft and out.

"Hostages are secured and ready to move," the company leader said.

Bastion stepped to him and his gauntlet landed firm on the man's shoulder. "May the Virtues guide you all in my stead."

"Cos protects us."

He spun around and, with the captives protected in the middle of their ranks, the company filed out.

Turning away to the tip of the spear, I shouted over the joint channel, "Advance!"

We left the harvesting chamber and raced onwards through narrow halls, corpse-filled antechambers, countless altars for Malnetha, and other vats, though we found no more living sacrifices. Within the black labyrinth, we only met a few dreadminds and lesser chimeras on our path, but they either fled or were cast aside by my blade, their reeking blood smeared on the decaying walls.

Our path shortly curved out to a high stony precipice. Sunken below was the largest cavern we'd come across yet. It was filled with burning flames and burrowed dens like a city of mounded houses. Dreadminds and other foul things scurried between, their raspy laughter and shrill screams echoing out across the lofty hollow. Yet amidst the tumult, I briefly caught faint chanting.

"Zorthan Illessar! Zorthan Illessar! Zorthan Illessar!"

A cosmos-shuddering growl answered the beckon and the entire cavern trembled. I forced everyone to a stop behind me as I gazed out, scanning for the source, but all I saw was a sea of dreadminds and their chimera pets, clambering across the cragged plain below, surging towards us.

I was tempted to use our remaining starfuse warheads to obliterate everything down there, but that was not our mission, nor had I been trained to forsake such a crucial weapon in our time of need. Time was one thing we were running out of.

"Malnetha drives them at us," Leonyd said.

"And it is our duty to drive them back!" Bastion yelled. *"Do not halt!"*

I shook my head out of a trance, then spared the raging swarm below one last look before I whipped around onto the path that led back into the wall of stone. The chanting and laughter fell away.

We shortly came to a deep ravine, over which a bridge had once spanned, but was now left in ruins on the edges. I leapt over first, with Leonyd close behind, then those in the second company followed with Bastion and the third company guarding the rear.

Once we were all safely across, the tunnel plunged down until it merged into a winding staircase, the steps sticky with red. Gilded statues guarded the wall side, while on my left, carved windows peered out into a large vertical shaft where glowing insects drifted like sacks of pulsating blood.

"Rier," I said as we continued circling down. *"What do you make of all this?"*

"These statues depict humans fighting against the Abhorrent Luug," she answered. *"I can still see glimpses of their true form beneath their defilement. I took a sample of a stone fragment; it is over three thousand years old, near when the Cold War finally ended."*

"I wonder if the Velutrans actually fought against them here?"

"I doubt it," Rier answered. *"If the Luug attacked this place, then nothing would have been left. That must be the only reason it survived that war and all the warring since. Well, that and because it's far beyond the borders of the*

Velutra. We seldom seek beyond the comfort of our territory these days."

"I can see why," Suchine remarked.

I hadn't gone that much further when Rier called out. *"Stop! There's something here."*

I reared to a standstill, trusting her judgement and specialised detecting equipment. Then I connected to her crystala feed and saw through her own eyes the golden statue of a man, both hands on the hilt of a greatsword that stabbed into the ground. Creeping down the man's face was a transparent blue blob, inside which were rainbow-coloured veins.

"No," she muttered. *"It can't be…"*

I stiffened. *"That can't be what I think it is. Rier?"*

"It's a sluugrall," she whispered in awe. *"What the Luug fed on when they were not devouring us, or entire worlds."*

"If the Luug never fought in this place, then how the caos is it here?" I said, transfixed on the blob's two soft points that formed a U, off which a small purple glob drooped as it searched for food.

"I do not know. Nor how the Zenlians haven't discovered it."

The Guild had come across cultists trying to resurrect the extinct Luug species more than once before; fortunately they never got far, either due to us, or a lack of genetic materials. But if that creature were to come into the right hands, then that terrible race which nearly wiped out all life in the galaxy could rise again.

"I need to take it back to the Mother Guild to study," she said, a greedy desire leaking from her mind. *"Then it can be destroyed."*

"It should be destroyed right now," I replied.

"This is for the Guild Mother to decide."

I growled, frustrated that we'd stopped again, and that Rier was challenging my command—but it wasn't truly mine. I hailed the Guild Mother with our discovery. *"Advise."*

A bloated silence followed, until she eventually answered. *"Collect the sluugrall. It shall be brought back to the Mother Guild for testing before its destruction."*

I shook my head in disapproval, but then hurried Rier on. *"We're leaving in five seconds. Make haste."*

She sent a mist up that dispersed around the creature and then pulled it off the statue, its wobbly form helplessly floating in that cloud. It returned to her crystala for safekeeping. *"It's secured. Proceed."*

Soon, the staircase ended and we passed out into a small square courtyard where a leafless tree of human corpses gently swayed in the musty air. The sky above was a burning green, save for a single black moon shining.

From somewhere in the shadows, I heard the Zenlians chuckling and chanting again. "Zorthan Illessar! Zorthan Illessar! Zorthan Illessar!"

"Pray give me the chance to silence their foul tongues," Leonyd snapped.

"You shall get your chance, brother," I said. *"Channel your anger into your sword."*

The foreboding sensation crept into my elan vital, their rhythmic chants pounding against my quickening heart, but I kept my ears open as their relentless singing grew louder. It gave me the clarity I needed.

"Zorthan Illessar! Zorthan Illessar! Zorthan Illessar!"

CHAPTER TEN

Zorthan Illesar

I quickened my pace, desperate to be gone from that foul place and to see the calm serenity of the stars once more. Desperate to accomplish our mission. Desperate to get every remaining Guilder to safety.

"There's an alternate route approaching," Carellus said. *"I scoured it from two of the last dreadminds."*

"What of the original path?" I questioned after my mind absorbed the route. *"It's far more direct to the Rebirth Doc and we cannot afford a delay. Do you now doubt it?"* *"I cannot certainly say. Zenlian lairs are festering with esoteric passageways. As it stands both shall lead us to our destination."*

"Then we keep straight," I said and sensed Bastion's leaking emotions confirm my decision.

We passed the alternate pathway to my right and pushed straight on through a short tunnel. Out the other side we spilled into a vast chamber, but as soon as I entered, a wall of deafening sound hit me. There was no laughter, just thousands of tormented voices screaming in agony—a *lullaby for the dreadminds*. I muted the horrible sound, and continued ahead.

The ceiling was of a grand height and it glimmered with stars as though we were back outside, crudely answering my wish. Passing rows of pillars in a blur, I managed to glimpse dying faces carved in them, fresh blood dripping from their eyes, and twisting mouths—the source of their collective death song.

Clinging to Cos' light, I raced down the ancient empty hall and my comrades followed, arrows of violet light cutting through the miserable gloom. It was then that my crystala suddenly went wild with detected movement.

"The swarm is pressing down on us!" Leonyd shouted.

Dreadminds, chimeras, and other feral spawns were swarming in from tunnels by the hundreds. Their chanting swelled like the coming of a great roaring flood, washing away everything in its path.

"Zorthan Illessar! Zorthan Illessar! Zorthan Illessar!"

At the rear of the company, Bastion was waving his blade, driving us on with deadly urgency. *"Malnetha itself pursues us! Move!"*

In the distance I discerned the faint white facade of a building, what I assumed to be an old Cos Temple long defiled. The carved stone appeared unnatural compared to the moon's bedrock that had composed most of the fortress thus far, and it still bore a good quality, unlike everything else that was crumbling with decay. Two circular cryglass windows glinted green either side of a tall arched doorway that was wide open and leaking a brooding bloody aura.

The scouts had cleared ahead—another abandoned altar of sacrifice—and proceeded through a narrow tunnel at the very rear which was our main route to reach the dungeons and Rebirth Doc. But as I burst inside, a veiled illusion was dispelled and the red glow vanished into a startling bright white. My legs screeched to a stop, as did those close behind me, and we all looked around in bewilderment. My assumption was correct. Wrapped around us were the clean walls of a Cos Temple.

It had been years since I'd been inside one. I had never been as devoted as Cosrick or some of my family. I got all the healing and repentance I needed while in ascension. Yet upon first glance, this temple was much the same as all the others I had visited.

Directly ahead in the centre floated the cosmic mirror—a large perfect sphere, half a pale green, the other a pure darkness, both ever shifting, ever vying for control over the cosmos. Behind that was an arched window the size of the entryway, countless irregularly shaped shards of cryglass depicting a cospriest in their full traditional garb, a glowing green sceptre in one hand, his other held atop his breast. Similar circular windows were placed all throughout, as were resplendent statues and rows of polished white stone seats.

"This can't be…" Leonyd murmured beside me. Rier, Suchine, and the others of my company moved inside, while the two other companies, including Carellus and

Bastion, remained outside, though they also halted as they now saw what we saw.

I'd only come to a brief stop before I started to notice the inconsistencies. There were finely carved Zenlian runes in the statues, the cospriest was bleeding tears, the multicoloured light pouring in through the windows swayed back and forth across the smooth temple floor, and in general, everything bore a lesser quality than it should have had, a mimicry of something great. I'd seen similar things before.

Against the vibrant colour of the temple, my attention was diverted down at my feet where a black circle with a cross through it had been carved into the ground. My chest tightened as I realised that the temple had been built—or restored—to torture the dreadminds with. They would be chained within the circle and forced to suffer all in the name of Malnetha, for all things we found beautiful tormented their cursed eyes.

"*Rier!*" I cried, directing my venom to her. "*What happened to our scouts?*"

"*They were destroyed right as we stepped inside. They must have been corrupted without me knowing as soon as they passed through.*"

Only then did I discern that the temple had no exit. No way forward.

"*We're trapped,*" Suchine rasped. Outside, the thousands of clamouring wretched spawns grew closer, echoing his hopelessness.

"*You've been proven wrong again, Mind Scourer!*" Leonyd cursed. "*This time to our ruin!*"

"I was not the one that brought us here," Carellus replied.

In that moment I realised our folly, but it was too late.

My head flicked up to the black and green sphere floating in the centre of the temple as it ruptured with a loud crack and a pale white light burst out, accompanied by a blood curdling scream. Pale hands and monstrous bones began clawing their way out through the widening folds of its womb.

Leonyd had his colossal rifle pointed straight at the emerging thing. *"Blast it back to the void!"*

The vibrant colours pouring in through the windows ceased, instantly replaced by a dark crimson as though the world outside had been murdered and the flood of blood was about to pour in. The cracking sphere was a blinding source of brilliant light, from which a dead and disfigured head slithered out, unleashing a gurgling scream so strong the entire temple shook.

"It's her," Suchine muttered as I too recognised her living corpse of a face. "Sagesworn Illesar."

"Zorthan Illesar," Carellus corrected.

"Caos," I breathed out, voice choked with despair. At that moment I failed as a leader. Stricken, I froze as though Malnetha itself had taken hold of my feet with its black claws. All I could do was hopelessly watch as the corrupted Sagesworn grew out the womb, bones snapping into place, rotting flesh folding in around her.

"What are we waiting for?" Rier shouted. *"Let's move!"*

"Where the caos are we going to go?" Leonyd spat.

"To the alternate path Carellus found!"

"So we can get trapped again?"

"Enough!" Bastion roared, giving us all the commanding presence we desperately needed. *"Back the way we came! Our mission is still the Rebirth Doc. We'll punch through the horde and take this new path. Out! Out! Out!"*

Before we could move, oozing holes opened all over Zorthan Illesar's contorting back, and out flew arrows of acidic blood, seeking missiles headed straight towards us. They crashed into four of the Guilders behind me, punching the head clean off one and blasting both legs off another, while the other two had massive holes torn straight through their chest, immediately sending them back to the Cos Realm.

Stretching further out of its womb to its true height, Zorthan Illesar screeched in awakening delight.

My dread burned away into the warrior Bastion had trained me to be. But I did not attempt to fight that thing there; above all else I sought to get my soldiers to safety, and no matter the threat, we never left any of our fallen behind.

I whirled around. *"Get the fallen and get out!"*

We did not have the time to absolve their bodies into our crystalas, so I grabbed the closest of my dead brothers by the arm and started to drag him out. Leonyd and the others did the same and we raced out of the temple right as Zorthan Illesar crashed onto the floor with a wet thud.

"Haste or die!"

Back out into the gigantic hall, a sea of dark shapes was flooding towards us, against which Bastion led the charge, his sword held high in defiance. More chittering chimeras and other vile things skittered out from high tunnels, teeth chomping as they crawled down the pillars of screaming faces. Louder than everything, the chanting continued.

"Zorthan Illesar! Zorthan Illesar! Zorthan Illesar!"

"There's too many of them!" Suchine howled.

At the tip of the spear, Bastion punched through the horde, battering everything out of his way, but he did not get very far before the momentum of his crystala was bogged down by the flood of enemies into a thick melee.

I lagged at the rear carrying our dead and wounded, the enemies swarming from every side. My crystala had formed quad guns suspended off my body and, operating on its own, wailed with constant blasts, but the swarm was so dense the guns did nothing to stop them from pressing forward. When I joined the rest of the huddled company standing their ground, I spun back, coalescing dual swords in my hands to fend off the crashing wave of enemies.

"Rock formation!" Bastion hailed.

Together, everyone merged their shields and a dim purple bulwark appeared over us, fending off the gnashing hordes. The thrashing dreadminds and chimeras caught inside were quickly cut down.

"Starfuse!"

I'd already used my starfuse warhead, and after we split our resources with the other companies, we only had three left. One of the Guilders tossed theirs up into the air above our shield and it wailed the deafening cry of a thousand undying wights before a light burst forth, and the entire hall trembled with a grumbling roar. Pure radiant starlight blinded everything for several seconds, and our joint shield shattered under the immense power, but it endured just long enough to keep us unharmed. When the light faded away, only a whirlwind of white dreadmind dust lingered.

"Onwards through their ashes!" Bastion bellowed.

Sprinting forward once more, we kicked up trails of the incinerated dead, but when we reached halfway down this long hall, a rapid blur crashed right into the middle of our group with a terrible thump and I reared to a halt in horror. Half of our soldiers were instantly crushed into puddles of their own blood and bone; others screamed and squirmed to get out from under the monster's five crushing legs.

From the wreckage of Guilders loomed a pale monstrosity. The beast was not distinctly human, save for the contorted dead face of the Sagesworn. Her enlarged eyes were filled with bubbling blood and her head was attached to the end of a long stalky neck, swaying this way and that. The monstrosity was staring straight down at me when it unleashed a howling roar like a dying mountain and then lunged forward.

I dodged out of the way with those nearby the best we could, but it caught two of them with a swing of its meaty weapons—masses of pulsating flesh and limbs as though it had ripped out its own organs and fashioned them into clubs—smashing my brothers into a shower of dissolved humans.

The Guilders on the flanks and behind fired up at the monstrosity to attract its attention, but it only enraged the thing into a frenzy, its clubs thrashing into the pillars and ground with thundering cracks. There was no running from this thing. It had a swiftness that was unnatural to its hulking, skeletal form.

Suchine darted out of the way and landed by my side, spinning his dual axes.

"Don't do anything rash," I rasped.

"That's something coming from you," Suchine replied.

"Throw everything at it!" I cried. "Avenge your fallen kin!"

I pointed my blade up at the thing and coalesced barrels along the edge. Side by side to Leonyd's howling rifle, we spewed out a swift hail of fire and all the remaining exploding cryorbs we possessed. Dancing cracks of white lightning banged one after the other, tearing off hunks of its rotten flesh and exposed bones, but the attacks did little against whatever cursed source of power gave it life. The trampling force of death came on with a flailing scream.

"Encircle it!" I roared. "Chain its limbs!"

"Pin the wretched thing down!" Bastion seconded.

Four soldiers on either side formed long chains, gleaming mosaics of radiant colour. They tossed them up and the chains wrapped around the Sagesworn's bent arms, then they desperately tried to drag them down to the ground. The thing wailed and stamped its many twisted legs in revolt.

Amidst the blurry flashes of our fire, I marked another six soldiers who were hacking at its legs from behind, but they were tall and hardened with senyar, making them difficult to cut through, especially as the legs came down like hissing bolts, smiting the ground with ruinous cracks.

Then I saw a Guilder blow one of its legs apart with her swinging mace, but the overgrown beast only recoiled for a second before it ceased its attack and convulsed in pleasure. All atop its back, flesh peeled apart to form white wings of flapping skin, yet it was the rotting black holes scattered all over that stole my focus.

I pinged everyone's attention. *"Incoming! Dodge!"*

A massive volley of blood arrows burst out from its holes and rapidly curved down upon us. Our shields were still on cooldown and as the acidic tracking missiles came straight for me, I leapt into the air, firing back as I went. When I crashed back down to the ground, I continued blasting up from a distance, but abruptly stopped as confused despair took over.

One of the missiles had punched a hole straight through Leonyd's chest. He collapsed to his knees, the violet cracks of his black armour dimming. Breathless, heartless, he spat blood and managed to send one last thought.

"I'm sorry, Rier," he said, that rough voice soft and broken in our minds. *"Teasing the Plague has finally caught up to me. I pray to Cos it doesn't drag you all down as well…"* His body fell forward with a hollow clang.

The coldness of Leonyd's light leaving my mind tore my elan vital in two and a wounded cry poured out of me from the very depths of my being. A vanquished sound I'd never made before. Brothers for over one-hundred and thirty years, ended just like that. I would give anything to hear one of his bold jests again, to feel that annoyance only a brother can stir in you.

"Leo!" Rier wailed as she rushed towards him.

Something inside me snapped. I soared forward off the ground, hot with fury. I had intended to put my blade straight into the Sagesworn's twitching head, but it vomited a shower of pestilence from that dead mouth and I darted away. I flew back at it again from a different angle and I poured all my crystala's strength into my blade as it smashed against its long, stretchy neck. I gripped the hilt of my sword tight as it ground against the hardened bone, my teeth rattling in my skull. Ultimately, my blade won and cut all the way through the bone with a shrill ring and the Sagesworn's dead face splattered on the ground, yet even then, it somehow continued shrieking in painful pleasure.

I careened back down to the ground, and was further disturbed to see that despite my removal of its head, and the chains holding its arms, the Sagesworn's body kept thrashing. Hiding on the edge of a nearby pillar, I marked Carellus eyeing the severed head greedily.

"Sister, stop!"

Heedless, she raced forward to scour its mind, but abruptly halted when the chains that were wrapped around the Sagesworn's arms finally cut through and its clubs fell to the ground with a heavy thud, exploding in great bursts of vile liquid that engulfed its own head, all the chain wielders, and several others whole.

Hopeless, I watched as they fell to the ground with the acid, reduced to a sizzling puddle in the blink of an eye—our only two remaining starfuses gone with them. The warmth of their presence extinguished from my mind, leaving a malicious silence. We had expected a fight, but not a slaughter.

"No!" It was all that made it out of my mouth. How pathetic that their deaths should accompany such a dull word in the halls of my memories. The horror rooted me where I stood.

I do not blame myself for their deaths. I don't blame anyone except Malnetha itself—even then. There is nothing to be done about such tragedies besides accept what was done, find forgiveness for yourself, make sure it doesn't happen again, and keep their memories alive. Leonyd was one of my closest brothers and centuries later I still carry his memory within my elan vital.

Suchine cried at the Sagesworn, shaking me free of my lamenting. The ground beneath me rumbled, the air sang with violence, and the bones within me trembled to flee. With its arms and head gone, I thought for a foolish moment that the Sagesworn was no longer a threat, but no. The beast was now unchained and still bore four legs and a hulking skeletal mass that blindly trampled around in a rampage, from the back of which blood-white projectiles periodically fired out.

Rier was kneeling on the edges of Leonyd's melted corpse as the Sagesworn came straight for her. Lost in her grief, I'd already seen her vulnerability and rushed forward, knocking us both out of the way.

As I did so, a cold impact of pain hit my arm like a meteorite. When we came to a stop, I gasped and stumbled. I reformed my blade into the ground to hold me upright and I snarled with the metal tang of blood in my mouth.

"Ludaan," Rier muttered, rattled. "Your arm."

Chest heaving, I looked down where my arm should have been but it was gone, a mangled stump in its stead. The pain dug its sharp bite into me before my crystala sealed it with a violet mist and pumped my veins full of nopaine serum, yet even then, a dull, ghostly ache remained for a long time after.

"Better mine than yours," I said, gritting my teeth, unable to speak the words aloud. Then I stood tall and swung my blade around. *"Gather yourself. Mourn later."*

I heard a violent growl ring out of her helm as it turned to face the Sagesworn. "Get out of my way so I can punish this wretch." She pushed me aside, reformed her rifle, and started blasting. "Your corruption ends now! Die! Die! Die!"

I turned in beside her, and together we unleashed a billowing hail of vengeance in Leonyd's name.

"Target its legs!" I called out, noticing pale white blood leaking from growing cracks.

Everyone concentrated their fire and the assailing blur of violet light intensified. The Sagesworn answered by spewing out another storm of liquid missiles, soaring all over until they butchered five more of our soldiers. We were all scattered across the centre of the hall now. Bastion and what was left of the other companies were further away towards the exit, firing everything they had at the beast, while Suchine had circled back around to me and Rier. Even Carellus was on the outskirts, using her crystala to fire black blasts from her hands.

There was no reprieve. The headless Sagesworn came straight for us again, but this time I hurled myself at it, my one remaining hand clenching my blade tight. It wanted to trample me, but I had other ideas. I quickly darted underneath its body, weaving between its stalk-ing legs, choosing my target carefully. Pouring every-thing I had left into my one blade, I swung until its edge screeched hard against one of its wounded legs, but still it was not enough and the impact knocked me to a halt.

The beast stamped on, reeling from the blow, but now diverted away from Suchine and Rier. As they continued firing, their blasts finally severed another of its hard skeletal legs—the one I had left a deep gash in—and the beast crashed into a pillar with a howling wail, smashing it into pieces and shaking the entire hall.

"Move while we can!" I shouted. Then I said something I'd never said before as I looked upon the white puddle where Leonyd had made his end. *"Leave the dead. Get out!"*

Even as I had the thought, the Sagesworn came hob-bling out of the rubble on its three mangled legs. Anoth-er wave of Zenlian spawns were crawling back into the hall from their hidden tunnels high above, their chants and laughter trickling in to start, quickly returning with a thundering vengeance.

"Zorthan Illesar! Zorthan Illesar! Zorthan Illesar!"

"Rally to me!" Bastion called. *"To me!"*

I waved Suchine and Rier on, and as they passed, I whirled around behind them, my crystala propelling me as fast as I could go.

The headless hulk of the Sagesworn kept on stumbling behind us, but now the scraps of flesh clinging to its skeletal form began merging in on itself—even those exposed bones started disintegrating.

"It's going to blow itself up!" I cried. *"Flee!"*

"Zorthan Illesar! Zorthan Illesar! Zorthan Illesar!"

The Sagesworn did not possess the strength to chase us any further and as it crashed to a halt, it released a guttural scream out of the sinking holes on its back and ruptured itself. An explosion of white ichor burst forth, flooding the hall with a gurgling torrent of corrosive blood, but the trails that launched into the air then funnelled into missiles racing down towards us.

I could see the exit tunnel almost within reach. Bastion stood by its side, waving everyone through, right as the rain of projectiles fell upon us. I twisted my body at the last second and one missile skimmed the side of my ribs, dissolving a shallow gash. Rier suffered a similar non-fatal blow, while Suchine and Carellus were missed completely, yet three other Guilders were smacked to the floor and left there to rot with gaping holes.

As I continued on, I saw Bastion had been knocked back against the wall, the side of his stomach missing as though a chimera had taken a hefty mouthful. I came to his side and poured some of my crystala to help the wound, the misty violet cleansing all of the dripping white acid.

He promptly pushed me away, breath wheezing. *"Save it for yourself! I can stand on my own."*

"Then move!" I ordered over the coming horde. They had finally ceased their chanting, but the cacophony of their ire grew louder.

"You don't command me just yet," Bastion snarled.

"Then command yourself out of here, fool!" I bit back in defiance. "Move!"

Clenching his stomach with one hand, he reformed a blade in his other and grimaced. "The light of Costhrall guides us. Always forward, Ludaan. Always endure."

With that he turned and fled into the tunnel, and I folded in behind him, the last to leave that cursed, forlorn hall, but as I did so a voice whispered, the cold words dancing inside my skull.

Zorthan Illesar.

CHAPTER ELEVEN

No Retreat

A hail from the Guild Mother cut through that ominous whisper. *"All companies retreat! Fall back! The mission is lost!"*

Data rushed through my mind of the onslaught on the fortress. The companies looking after the hostages were completely wiped out. That alone would have broken me on any other day, but all the tragedy was starting to blur into one all-encompassing fog of sorrow.

Overall, the Guild's strength had been reduced in half and the Guild Mother was unwilling to lose any more of her soldiers for a mission we had still not yet achieved. The only good news was that Zenli, Her cursed self, had not arrived, yet Malnetha kept piling on us.

"We have no way back," Bastion answered the Guild Mother. The courtyard we had originally come through was now overrun with chimeras rushing straight for us, giving us no other option than to turn down the alternate route Carellus had previously discovered.

"The escape tunnel," Carellus suggested. *"We proceed to the dungeons and come out the other side of the moon."*

Rier objected. *"We don't even know if it's real. Your scourings have only led us astray this far. We are but nine left."*

"We will be far fewer if we face that horde," Bastion conceded. *"Our only way forward is away from them. For now we must place our trust in the information from the dreadminds and*

continue to the dungeons. Guild Mother, send a transport to the pinged location to await our collection."

"It shall be there," the Guild Mother replied. *"Just make sure you get there alive, Bastion. This day is already too black."*

I rushed after the others down a corridor, blocking out that feeling of having a part of myself destroyed—limbs could always be regrown. But I could never regrow the emptiness from the death of my comrades.

Floating thick in the air were virulent yellow spores just waiting for the opportunity to seep in through our crystalas and sizzle our insides or corrupt us into something worse.

"We're heading straight into a nest," Suchine said.

"It's empty all the way to the grav-sheath," Rier answered.

"That doesn't help."

Rier had sent scouts ahead to clear the way and to begin hacking the grav-sheath that would carry us to the dungeons, though they'd yet to reach their destination, giving me little comfort, especially after our last ones had deceived us. We'd already learnt the hard way how the Zenlians could surprise us, but life is never-ending in its brutal lessons.

Four dreadminds leapt out in front of Rier from a collapsed hole in the ceiling, their pale rotting flesh gleaming in the dark. Two lifted their rifle-infused arms and fired at her, while the other two laughed maniacally and leapt forward with their curved knives, but she was quicker. Stronger. The blasts screeched off her armour, as did the enemies' blades, and she thrust her own forward into the chest of one, while her left hand caved in the throat of the other. Suchine, who was closest behind her, tossed his axes forward and they curved around her, chopping off the heads of the other two dreadminds.

"Shifty little wretches," Rier spat as I came up beside her and the corpses thudded to the ground.

Her drained eyes met mine. *"We're almost there."*

The echoing laughter of the pursuing horde urged me on and I took the lead once more, Rier, Suchine, and Carellus right on my tail. Bastion came next, his weary face on the verge of passing out from the massive gash taken out of his stomach, yet his crystala still matched our speed, while four other Guilders guarded the rear.

Other passageways started appearing off our main corridor, a dizzying maze according to Carellus' schematics. Whichever way we went, the spores only intensified and were accompanied by large pulsating pustules that oozed yellow bile as we trampled them on the floor—fortunately their acid was not crystala-piercing like the Sagesworn's or the shellhounds'. Between the fleshy and putrid growths, black holes like gaping mouths became more frequent.

Out of nowhere, a voidshield spawned right in front of Bastion, the wall of transparent shadows blocking his path. I screamed to a halt, spinning back around aghast with shock. As I rushed forward to attack the shield, explosions triggered in the ceiling with a warped crack, and the stone came crumbling down. I lurched backwards, the collapsing ceiling making me retreat further and further. When it eventually stopped, so did I, and I scowled up at a wall of rubble now cutting us off from one another.

"We're alive," Bastion said, and I saw through our connection that he and the four Guilders stood on the other end of the collapsed corridor.

"Cut through it," I ordered, madly gesturing forward to the other three beside me. *"Quickly!"*

"No time," Bastion responded. *"They're coming."*

The horde was pressing closer now, and I felt the vibration rattling through the wall of stone.

"Take this path," Carellus said, highlighting the route in our minds. *"It links up to the grav-sheath."*

"Haste!" I cried, chains of dread squeezing my heart tighter. *"We'll wait for you there! Always forward! Always endure!"*

"You don't have my permission to die just yet, Bastion!" Rier shouted.

We were off, Rier, Suchine, and Carellus right behind me, together a deadly blur of violet. Gliding forward, I anxiously watched in a corner of my mind as

Bastion and the others desperately raced on, but they did not get far before a swarm of chimeras crawled out of tunnels in front of them, blocking their path forward.

"They're on us!" one of my brothers cried out as he leapt forward, hacking into their pale flesh.

"We're surrounded!" yelled another at the rear. He spun around, firing a constant stream of purple misery at the main advancing horde.

"Drown them in the rain of their own vile ichor!" Bastion howled, lost in battle fervour as he ripped a chimera's head off and crushed another with his foot, before pumping four others in quick order with his gun. He stumbled to his knees from his stomach wound, but the other warriors fended off the enemies long enough for him to give a defiant cry and he lunged back into the melee.

One of the Guilders at the rear was separated by the surging chimera horde, and the things leapt all over him, picking at their meal, and he yelped and pleaded as they dragged his body down their ranks, tearing limb from limb.

"Hold out!" All I could do was helplessly watch as I raced forward. *"We're coming!"*

"Leave!" Bastion roared. *"That's an order! Go on without us!"*

"Curse your orders. I'm not leaving you behind!"

As I advanced, that insidious phantasm washed through me like a cold breeze, and I sensed it creeping through the walls, its blazing green eyes narrowing on the hunt. But I was not its target. The heavy pressure in the air receded like a fleeting shadow, dragging its malice away—towards Bastion.

"Focus on the edge of your sword!" I said to Bastion, though I knew right then that the phantasm was no mere illusion, but something true and born with otherworldly malevolence.

Even in thought, Bastion's words came soft, yet confident. *"Ludaan, you have to keep going. Leave us."*

"Shut up!" I cursed, frantically racing down that blackened corridor, yellow spores dispersing in my path. I'd shot ahead of the others. Everything was blind to me except saving Bastion. "I will not abandon you."

Chimeras leapt all over the soldier beside Bastion, too many for him to shake off, and he was pinned to the ground, their ghastly teeth sending up spurts of blood and scraps of flesh as they devoured him. The others hewing at the horde were overcome a second later, their final screams warbled as their tongues were ripped out. The rest of the chimeras were twitching back and forth, edging closer to Bastion, but hesitating.

"There's something else in here," Bastion muttered. *"The phantasm…I can feel it peering through the walls, it's piercing me."*

The horde jerked to a halt, falling deathly still and silent. Bastion spun around, clenching his wound with one hand, his hilt with the other, pointing the tip of his sword at his foes. Then they slowly crawled backwards into the shadows, hissing.

"You wretched cravens!" he spat. "Give me a proper death!"

Silence.

In their place, the heavy thuds of wet sloshing footsteps and eight burning green eyes came to grant him his wish.

Bastion stood tall, resolved. Then he sent me these words, *"I'm proud of you, my son. Carry on Costhrall's light for us all."*

The blazing emerald eyes lurched forward and my connection went black, the light of Bastion in my mind cold.

The impact of his death stopped me right there and I crumbled to my knees as though I had joined the dead. My ragged breath caught in my throat as if the vacant void had forced its way in, choking. I tried to rationalise it as another Zenlian deception, but I'd already lost too many others for it not to be true.

Some part of me thought Bastion was immortal like the Rebirth Doc we were hunting—I suppose all sons think of their fathers in that way. But that was foolish. He was just a man, albeit brave and strong-minded, but still just a human; a thing of flesh and bone, held together by the grace of Costhrall, now forever returned to the Great Ocean Above.

Life has meaning when living, that is true, but it is only solidified in death—forever fused into the currents of the cosmos. Bastion's bravery, his sacrifice, still lives on in memory, in me and whoever hears this. Only when he is truly forgotten does the meaning of his life completely vanish, though even then, I have to believe that some part of his memory is stored within the fabric of the universe and that he will be reborn anew. Just like all the other fallen.

I don't know how long I knelt there lost in grief. The next thing I remember is Suchine pulling at me, his muffled voice distant. "Ludaan, get up! We have to move!"

I blinked and flashes of violet light were all around me, screaming down the corridor into the dark. I heard the blasts squelching against the coming chimeras before I saw them.

"Get up!" Rier shouted over her wailing dual rifles. "You are the Guild's sword! An emissary of Costhrall and justice! Get up, brother!"

Suchine hit me in the back of the helm but it was his words that brought me back. "We must avenge Bastion! Do not let his death be for nothing!"

Snarling, I reformed my blade and stabbed it into the ground, then I pushed myself up. My battle senses snapped back and I knew we could not make a stand in this coffin of a corridor. I knew that I had to do everything I could to get the others out of here alive.

"Flee!" I knocked Rier's weapons out of the way to stop her from firing and pushed her on. "Move! Move!" Then we darted away towards the grav-sheath with the chimeras close on our heels.

As we went, I heard a faint voice trilling out from the burrows.

"The Zenlian mother is coming. She will deliver Malnetha's delight to all."

It took me a second to realise it was Bastion's voice, but I did not stop. I did not let the doors of my sanity crack any further.

Then there was a human baby crying. An old man cackled with laughter. Cosrick and Leonyd screamed in agony as though they were being tortured to speak. The rest of my dead soldiers joined in until it was a roaring cacophony of chasing sobs, laughter, and wails. The mounting madness tried to drag me down into Malnetha, but I did not stop.

"Our minds are as hard as senyar!" I cried. "Do not let Malnetha in!"

We flew this way and that throughout the labyrinth, but the path quickly became so bloated with blubbery pustules that we had to slow down as only one of us could fit through at a time, their leaching yellow bile brushing against what was left of my crystala.

Rier was at the front of our group, hacking at them as she went. *"I'm going to obliterate this entire caosing moo n."* *"We will get our vengeance, sister,"* I bitterly promised.

Amongst the disorder of my mind, the Guild Mother's words came to me. *"You bring them home, Ludaan. Bastion watches over you."*

"On his name I swear I'll see it done," I answered.

The pustules eventually came to a sudden stop, their growth confined to the hallway, and we shot out into a wide circular chamber. Right in the centre fell a massive dark pit—the shaft that would carry us all the way down to the dungeon and Rebirth Doc. There was a path on the opposite side but going below was now our only way out, that is if the tunnel Carellus had discovered really was true. I had no time to think otherwise.

I shuddered as my feet landed back on the ground. It was covered in crammed faceless corpses all slithering about. I reminded myself the best I could that they were contained by some kind of cryglass; the same was true for the walls and flat ceiling, but it did little to comfort my repugnance.

"Why isn't the grav-sheath ready?" I demanded of Rier.

A chandelier of dead faces dangled above the pit, their limp visages covered in throbbing blue veins. Violet mists swirled all around it—the scouts Rier had sent ahead turned into hacking instruments.

"The system is rotten with contagions," she cursed. *"I need another minute."*

I peered back at the bleeding pustules at the end of the tunnel, the rumbling of the coming horde getting closer. "We don't have a minute!" I shouted, gripping my blade tight. *"Carellus, help her cleanse the contagions. All of you, cast your shields against that main tunnel. We have to hold them off as long as possible."*

I raised my translucent barrier, blocking the passage, and the others added theirs, fortifying it. Then the four of us repositioned in a line with our backs facing the edge of the pit, our eyes staring down our coming doom.

"We can't hold them off," Suchine moaned. *"You've seen what they've done. There are too many of them."*

"Silence your doubts," I snapped. I wouldn't let myself or anyone else think defeatist thoughts. That would

certainly mean our demise. *"Rier, as soon as you have control over the grav-sheath you pick us up and shoot us down, understood?"*

I turned to Suchine. His hands trembled on the grips of his dual axes; his eyes shook with pain and fear. A sliver of regret knifed at my heart for bringing him into the Guild, to his impending demise, yet in the end he displayed his true quality.

"Caos it," he spat. "You're right. I'm going to make these vile beasts bite the edge of my sword. They will cower against the light of Cos." He spun his axes, the lusting eagerness for battle growing. "Whether it's here today or a hundred years away. I'm dying beside my family in battle."

I bitterly smiled at that. "Don't be so reckless."

Summoning another blade, I had it replace my destroyed arm. As I swung it around, some of my lost confidence returned. I couldn't afford to make the same mistakes. Arm or not, I would fight until my very last breath.

"Here they come!"

The horde tore through the pustules filling the tunnel and crashed against our shield with a booming crack. The chimeras gnawed against our bulwark with their fangs, but it held strong.

"Illuminate them with Cos' light!"

With our combined crystalas, we formed a turret right in front of us, four long barrels ready to belt anything in its path. Spewing out a constant screech of fire, the blasts passed through our aligned shield, squashing the bugs with a melody of shrill dying cries. Their minced corpses quickly filled up the tunnel, but the mindless spawns were relentless and kept coming, tearing at their own dead just to get ahead.

"Rier!" I impatiently yelled.

"*Thirty seconds!*" she answered, nervously bouncing a long spear between her hands.

"*You think our shield has that long left?*"

"*We're doing our best!*"

"*The roots of corruption go deep,*" Carellus added.

We poured more and more of our crystala to keep the turret going, even though it meant our armour was being drained. We reduced its spurting fire to intermittent bursts, as the chimeras slowed through the narrow opening packed with their deliquesced dead.

"The shield is faltering," Suchine cried. "Get ready!"

The barrier shattered with a warped bang and true terror coursed through my veins like never before.

A sea of white slush poured into the chamber, and flowing in with it were the writhing mass of pale creatures. The turret kept firing until the last second right before the chimeras swarmed it when we recalled it back to our crystalas.

Upon the edge of the grav-sheath's pit, we stood our ground. The barrels on my blade were howling as the horde advanced, exploding their bony limbs off in hunks, yet their strength was always in numbers. In crawling over their dead.

"Decimate their blackened hearts!" I roared as the enemy crashed into us.

I thrust my blade through the chest of the first chimera to get in range, then tossed it aside while my other blade cleaved one in half with a downward strike, its hot white blood spraying everywhere. I kicked a leg off another that was close with a wet crunch, then my sword swept around, severing its head. I slashed and hacked and kicked and punched and shot every ravenous cursed spawn that mindlessly flung itself at us.

Weary beyond belief, my chest heaved, ragged bits of spit and blood leaking from my mouth. Pain continually crept back into my remaining arm, into my other wounds with a blazing vengeance. The black armour of my crystala withered away blow after blow, revealing the silver senyar plates fixed to my flesh below.

I eventually forsook my second blade in favour of defence; even then, my one sword was dim and had shortened almost into a knife. It didn't matter how many I killed. All I had to do was hold out until the grav-sheath was ready.

Cackling, a delirium of dreadminds entered the fray, storming through the lesser chimera horde, sparing even them no mercy. I cleaved through the first one, but the third one that leapt at me had a single eye on her stitched-together face, and it cracked wider, the veins pulsing just like the last two times. Then Malnetha bust the doors of my sanity wide open.

Berserk, I thrust my blade into that watching eye and then I kept stabbing even when there was nothing left. I furiously gouged all the eyes of the dreadminds that came at me, even the lifeless eyes of the chimeras were expunged in my frenzy. Lost in madness, I was about to thrust my blade through Rier's back when a deep droning sound reverberated out of the tunnel, pulling me out of my rampage. The swarm stalled their assault, convulsing in ecstasy above their eviscerated kindred.

"What the caos is that?" Rier muttered.

The same coldness that had passed through me on its way to Bastion did so again, but now it lingered, its icicles stabbing my heart. "That thing with the burning eyes," I growled. "The phantasm."

"We're next," she said on a faltering exhale.

"The thing can't have us!" Suchine roared and he tossed his axes into the stalled chimeras, spinning by themselves in a long arc, butchering everything in their way until they snapped back into his hands.

I spun away from Rier, from almost killing one of my best friends, and slit the throat of the wretch closest to me, then punched the head off another. *"Get control of this sheath!"*

"We're almost there!" Rier answered.

The horde screamed and thrust themselves back at us, the same choir of madness now coming from the tunnel on the opposite side of the grav-sheath. We were wholly surrounded with only one way out.

Death.

Despite our imminent demise we kept fighting with all our might, but it was not enough. Carellus yelped as she had her legs dragged out from under her and the chimeras surged on top, ripping her to shreds.

"Sister, no!" my voice rang out but it was deadened by the tumult. I cut a wretch in half and went to rush forward to her aid, but the chimeras latched onto my back and my own legs, holding me in place. I thrashed, trying to shake, stab, and blast them off, but more kept leaping on, their claws scratching at my armour, digging in through its thin cracks.

The last I ever saw of Carellus were the golden rings on her fingers as she reached out for help. I failed her. I broke the promise on Bastion's name. Yet I still had two more promises to break.

I writhed free of the chimeras holding me back, allowing me to glimpse one as it plunged its fangs into Rier's neck and she wailed out in pain, blood gushing, yet she grabbed its throat with one hand and snapped its neck, dropping the body before three more jumped on. Beside her, and with his axes and crystala worn away, Suchine madly thrashed, his bare fists held out by six chimeras gnawing at his arms on either side.

I bellowed and let my enemies have what fury I had left, summoning every ounce of rage and strength to get to my comrades, but it was not enough. I could not move. They stabbed, scratched, and bit me all over, and I gushed blood and howled in the purest agony I'd ever felt. The acrid scent of death burned my lungs. It was like my elan vital was being torn in half and I'd never return to the Cos Realm.

Never has such hopelessness ruined me as it did at that moment. All my training, all those dedicated years proved useless. We meant nothing to Malnetha. We were simply prey.

Through the jumbled frenzy of slaughter, I caught a glimpse of something emerging from the tunnel. It had a similar pale colour and distorted human figure to the swarming slaves but it stood upright on two slender arms, and its swollen stomach bore eight eyes afire with a sickly emerald.

Bastion's dead voice whispered in my mind. *"Your flesh will replenish my children."*

The phantasm was no longer merely an apparition, but the creature treading towards us. It caught me in its gaze again and thrust an ethereal blade of ice through my heart, one I could not pry free with all my might. It twisted my veins, scratched at my bones, tormented me with visions of committing murder upon my brothers and sisters. It made me revel in the thoughts of fratricide. It was my master and did not know mercy.

I would have given into Malnetha right then and there if it meant Rier and Suchine could live, but the cosmic clutch of the grav-sheath yanked me off the ground, crushing all the chimeras around me into a flood of pale white blood. The world became a blur and the next thing I knew, I was standing atop the transparent lines of the sheath, silently plummeting down the lightless shaft to the centre of the moon.

When I drew in a deep breath, I noticed the cold presence of the phantasm had retreated, not defeated but dissatisfied. I turned to see Rier and Suchine kneeling beside one another gasping and ragged, but both still alive, and a beam of starlight uplifted my vital.

I rushed over and gave them the dregs of my crystala, helping seal the wound on Rier's neck and Suchine's mutilated arms, while warm blood trickled down my ribs and legs.

"Hold on," I said, voice heavy with exhaustion. I wanted them to hear it from my own mouth. "We're getting out of here."

"I'll believe it when I see it," Rier muttered, forcing herself to stand, but I extended my arm to hold her upright. Her helm had worn away, revealing her dark hair matted with blood. *"Twenty seconds until we hit the bottom."*

"Enough time for some quick shut-eye?" I said with a wry grin, hiding my own fear; hiding the truth of my company's slaughter. I would not spend my last moments grieving for the fallen. I would honour their deaths by protecting those who were left. If we ever made it out of there alive, then and only then would I let myself grieve.

"Out of the void and into the black heart," Suchine said, and I heard the exhaustion in his thoughts, though he was not yet defeated.

"Oh, I'm hopeful things won't be as bad down here," I replied, answering the old adage.

Rier grimaced and she pushed me away to stand on her own. *"I don't think I've ever heard you use the word 'hope' before."*

"I've never been in the depths of a Zenlian dungeon with one arm and two lunatics at my side."

That got a smile out of her. Then I hailed the Guild Mother. *"We're about to reach the dungeons and make for the exit. Status on our transport?"*

"We just witnessed a small fleet of voidcrafts fleeing from there. The escape tunnel exists." The Guild Mother answered, and a ray of hope warmed the icy wound the phantasm had left. *"They destroyed two of the vessels I sent, but one remains hidden away until you are ready. It is all that can be spared. Forgive me, Ludaan, but the Mother Guild can't hold here any longer. We have to ascend now."* There was a pause in her words that said everything. *"May the Virtues guide you all in my stead."*

"Cos protects us," I answered.

"They've left us," Suchine murmured.

"I would do the same. Too many have already perished." I lifted Suchine to his feet. "We can do this. We rush the escape route. Whatever happens, we stick together."

"Maybe dance with a few more dreadminds on the way out?" Suchine chuckled, then coughed a few times between wheezy breaths.

I mirrored his grim smile. It's something Leonyd would have said.

"And the Doc?" Rier questioned.

"You heard the Guild Mother. The mission has failed. All I care about now is getting you two out of here alive."

"What if he's still down there and alive?" Then she smiled weakly. *"Maybe we can force him to bring everyone back."*

"Don't talk like that," I snapped. *"Not even as a jest. You mar their sacrifice, their honour. If they were to be Reborn, then what meaning would their choice carry?"* Rier looked at me hard. *"None, but at least they'd still be alive."*

"If you live without meaning then you have already died." I still think that is true today, even after everything.

Rier scowled and shook her head.

I spun around, wanting to grip the hilt of my blade tight, but my crystala was gone. All I had left was my one fist, two legs, and my elan vital that was resolved to live.

"Focus, we're at the bottom."

CHAPTER TWELVE

Prisoner

The grav-sheath spat us out into a darker shade of black as though the night itself smothered us with its stark touch.

Inside my mind, I followed the route of the blue line throughout the dungeon labyrinth to the escape tunnel carved out of the dead moon's heart. The location of the imprisoned Rebirth Doc was marked nearby on a diverted path, but that no longer mattered. The only thing on my mind was getting Rier and Suchine to safety. We did not have far to go.

"We move quickly and quietly," I said.

I realised I could not hear the laughter of dreadminds, not the rustle of a breeze, not even the shudders of our own breaths. An unnatural silence stole all sound as though we were back in the void, yet I felt the hot stagnant air that burned my chest with every short inhale. It made me want to retch.

"What is this silence?" Suchine whispered in thought.

"Clear it from your mind," I replied. *"Focus on putting one step forward in front of the other."* I looked at Rier and

Suchine one last time, lending them the false fortitude in my eyes. *"We don't stop for anything, understand? You both stay right at my tail. Are you ready?"*

They both nodded.

The route in my mind led me on in the darkness where my eyes failed. Our footsteps muted, we slowly stalked through a labyrinth of interconnected prison cells littered with corpses and left behind experiments—only discernible by the faint violet glow of the crystala scraps holding Rier and Suchine's injuries together. The further we went, the deeper a foreboding crept into my heart and the quicker I picked up the pace.

Sweat beaded off my skin, mingling with the blood leaking out of my open wounds. My weak legs kept wanting to crumble and my head spun in dizzying circles on the verge of losing consciousness, yet by the strength of my elan vital I kept going.

"Where are all the dreadminds?" Suchine wondered.

"Guild Mother says they've fled, remember?"

"That or they were called above," Rier added. *"Either way, there's nothing left down here."*

A part of me was thankful that we couldn't afford to send out scouts. Sometimes it was worse knowing what lay ahead. For now we had hope, and that was enough to keep going.

A shrill scream cut through the unnatural silence in the distance.

"Did you hear that?" Suchine asked, fear mingling with my own. *"Or have I already lost my mind?"*

"I heard it too," I said.

"So much for nothing down here."

"At least we'll fall to Malnetha together," Rier grimly quipped.

I kept putting one foot forward in front of the other as I had told Suchine. *"It's probably just another prisoner or thrall left to rot. Keep going."*

We hadn't made it far when around the next corner we stopped before a tall arched doorway illuminated in glaring green runes. *"No, it can't be…"*

"That's the door to the Rebirth Doc," Rier said. *"What's it doing here?"*

Suchine stopped beside me. *"Carellus' schematics have failed us once more."*

"Or led us to complete our mission," I said, the symbols burning my unprotected eyes. I looked over my shoulder then through the routes in my mind. *"There's no other way forward. The escape tunnel might be through there. We have to go on."*

There were no objections. We had nowhere else to go. I stepped through. When the glare of the runes settled, I looked up at a tall throne of black cryglass. A pale man sat at the peak, eyes closed and motionless, his wrists and ankles bound to the chair with shifting shadows. The only light in this place came from ourselves and a red crescent moon hanging above the throne, leaking trails of blood.

"He looks dead but I cannot help fear otherwise," Rier said.

Suchine stumbled forward. *"The Sagesworn must have had him killed before dealing with us."*

I scanned the surroundings but there were no other paths, just the throne enveloped by nothingness. The sound of my own breath came back strangely to my ears and I wondered why this place was free of the all-pervasive silence.

A coughing fit overcame Suchine and he collapsed to the floor, retching blood. "I think those foul little things got to me," he sputtered.

I rushed down to his side, cradling his head. "It's gonna take more than that to kill you. Just hold on." His only answer back was coughing up more blood on me.

"There's no way out!" Rier wept *"Where the caos do we go?"*

"Anywhere but here!" I spat back at her and as I did so my eyes flicked up to the man atop the throne as his shot open.

"My saviours," he whispered.

Crimson chains burst out of the ground and wrapped around my arm, dragging me to my knees and locking me in place. Rier was dragged down just the same and both of us struggled to no avail. Helpless and trapped. Suchine was lifted up and forced to the same kneeling position, but his head dangled down unconscious. Rier abruptly joined him as though a serum had instantly placed her into sleep, but my eyes gaped across in horror, wide awake.

Heedless of my futility, my chest heaved as I thrashed and screamed. I hailed the Guild Mother, anyone else for help, but my thoughts were blocked from reaching out.

The man stood from his throne, his scrappy thin hair swaying about his broad shoulders. "Just when you think you have a plan, causality comes along and kicks you down."

"What did you do to them?" I growled, aching with uncertainty.

"No need for fear," he said, waving a hand. "They're still alive—at least for now. They won't remember any of this, nor perhaps shall you." He slunk down the steps with a casual playfulness, his thin pale limbs draped in black tattered robes. "Ah, millennia of memories swim in this pitiful container and yet I've forgotten a terrible amount."

"Millennia?" The word pierced my mind, infesting it with despair. "You wretched thing. Rebirth can't save you from me. I'm going to erase you."

I could see his grin beaming against the black throne as he cascaded down the steps like a waterfall. When he reached the ground, his smile vanished and he paused, gazing away for a long, distant moment, a gleam of yearning in his light green eyes.

I don't know what thoughts were going through his blackened mind, but I knew the terror that twisted mine. My mantra came to me; anything to deny my death—my failure. *I've faced death countless times. I'll face death countless more. My crystala is my sword and shield. Costhrall flows through my elan vital granting me strength. Costhrall lends me its light to blind the darkness. I've faced death countless times. I'll face death countless more. My—*

He turned back to me with that cold grin. "Aren't introductions normally the custom with conversations? Don't you want to know my name?"

"I don't give a caos!"

"I've taken many for myself over the years," he blithered, heedless of my hatred. "But I doubt you'd be interested in those. It's one name in particular that I've been given which I believe you would recognise." He paused, gently biting his bottom lip. "The Plague."

I gasped. "The Plague?"

"A name given to me by Empress Zenli, Her cursed self." The Plague scoffed, then chuckled. "Flattering, isn't it, Ludaan?"

"You know my name?" I muttered, stunned. There I was, kneeling before an immortal deity, every passing second descending into a new threshold of dread.

"Why, I know more about you than your own self." The Plague strode towards Suchine, looming above his bowed head. He turned to me, one of his pale green eyes opening wide, the veins pulsating. "I've been watching you."

"You," I breathed out, my entire body shivering. "You were watching me through those eyes—through the dreadminds."

"You should be glad," he said. He tilted his head and the eye returned to normal. "You weren't falling to Malnetha after all."

"I'll be glad when you're dead!"

The Plague went quiet as he ignored me and eyed Suchine with an air of deference. He slowly knelt beside him and, reaching out, gently caressed his black curly hair.

I squirmed against my restraints. "Don't touch him!"

He gestured to my shackles. "You're in no position to command me."

"Leave him alone!"

"You have come to deeply care for the boy, and he you. Loyal comradery, what a beautiful thing." The Plague clicked his tongue, and his poisonous eyes snapped to me. "He doesn't have long left to live. I wonder what depths of grief your mind will sink to when he dies, just like the rest of your company, just like all those that are still out there dying."

"I'm going to rip out your tongue and feed it to the dreadminds," I snarled, seething.

He shook his head. "An admirable rage. Alas, useless here." He let go of Suchine, straightened and stepped over to me. "Futility is a great tool for humility. It cleanses the elan vital of all its hubris, all of Malnetha's primal corruption, all that makes you rotten. Well, that or it breaks the mind and you become one of its pathetic slaves."

The more he spoke, the more it didn't make sense. There was no doubt a madness about him, but despite being in the depths of a Zenlian dungeon with an immortal Rebirth Doc, I could not grasp him as being mad like the dreadminds. No, this was a different kind of madness.

Then something clicked. "You lured us here, didn't you?"

"You?" He raised his eyebrows, then started pacing back and forth. "Oh, Cos no. You pesky Rebirth hunters just happened to get here first. Turns out nothing has changed in the Guild for half a century."

"Liar," I growled. "You revelled in watching all of them get slaughtered, didn't you? Like we're nothing. You're sick."

"I didn't ask you to assault this fortress," the Plague said, and a look that might have been concern flashed across his face. "Nor did I command any dreadmind or chimera to slaughter your soldiers."

I did not believe a word, but I rancorously questioned him, wanting to expose his lies. "What about that wretched phantasm?"

He scrunched up his face as though he'd taken offence. "Void, no. I've stayed clear of that ghastly thing. I need not lecture you on the strangeness of Malnetha's manifestations." His expression hardened again as he stopped pacing and faced me. "I'm afraid you have me all wrong. I'm simply trapped between two warring forces, waiting for the beloved Empress Zenli. I went to all this trouble for Her."

My worthlessness quickly dawned on me. Whatever was going on was far larger than the Guild, than myself, but I never cowered from that which terrified me and so I spat at his feet. It was all I could manage. "You're no different to all the other wretches that worship Her."

The Plague barked a laugh. "Worship? You are mistaken, Ludaan. I want the same as you do, as the entire Velutra does." He paused, leaning in so close I felt his icy breath. "I want Her dead. I will crush Zenli into the void so deep not even Malnetha will be able to find Her."

I stayed silent in my confusion, but I quickly came to learn that the Plague hated silence and would fill it with his conniving voice.

"I've been waiting here days and nights for Her to arrive," he said, then he gritted his teeth and growled. "I've been waiting centuries to end our battle. But your Guild has set me back once more."

I leered at his face right in front of mine. "Sorry to disappoint."

"Alas, your apology will not remedy all the suffering she will continue to inflict on this galaxy."

He pulled away, standing tall. I was certain death was coming for me then. I supposed that's why I stalled and asked, "Why do you want to kill Her?"

He showed me his back and spoke softly up to that false bleeding moon. "I am Her bane and she is mine."

"That does not answer my question."

The Plague's thumbs flicked out of his closed fists three times. "I am not the one whose liberties are currently on hold." He turned back around, his solemn countenance fixated on me. "I see your being, Ludaan, I see the strand that connects you to the Cos Realm above. I see your elan vital."

I groaned, shaking my head. "You're mad."

"I am nothing like them," he said, tilting his head up to the emptiness. "No, I'm more like you, just a little different."

"You're nothing like me!" I yelled, gritting my teeth.

His thin smile gleaned down. "We're all just rivers drifting away from our oceanic home." He stretched out his hands and a projection of a pale green river appeared. Admiring it, he continued speaking while his hands danced through the mist. "Such a fragile thing, the elan vital. I'm surprised to see one so strong." His reverence vanished along with the projection, and those cruel green eyes snapped back to me. "Life is fair in that it is unfair to everyone."

There was so much about Rebirth technology that we didn't know, hence this mission, but if he could see the strength of an elan vital—if such a thing were even true—then I wondered what use he had for mine. I certainly didn't feel like it held any strength left.

"So what?" I grumbled. "You're going to corrupt my vital and use me as a tool for your battle against Zenli?"

The Plague glided closer. "Causality has brought you to me, and I am not one to waste such a fine opportunity." His smile deepened again, this time with a glowing viscousness. "How would you like to live forever?"

"You mock me."

"You need only accept the offer."

"Caos off!" I swore. "Even if you speak the truth, I don't want it! Living forever is a curse."

"Oh, I'm well aware. One day even I shall finally lay down to rest." He stepped over to Rier and, bending down, fiddled with the ends of her knotted hair. Then his eyes narrowed and he reached down under her breastplate, rummaging.

"Get your hands off her!"

"Ah, here it is," he said, and he pulled out the transparent blue blob that was the sluugrall, admiring it in the palm of his hand. "I best keep this. We don't want it falling into the wrong hands now. Wouldn't want the Luug coming back, would we?" He tucked it into a fold of his tattered robes and returned his attention to me. "Tell me, do your comrades echo your beliefs about immortality?"

I bit my tongue, not wanting to waste anymore words with him.

"What about all those who have died today?" he continued, too calm for my liking. "Do you think they share your sentiment in the Cos Realm? You're right. They're dead. You're not. Neither is your friend here." His head whipped back to Suchine, who awoke startled before violently convulsing and retching more blood. "Although I have an inkling that his time is running out."

I winced as I looked at Suchine. There was nothing I could do for him. I wanted to plead with the maniac before me, but I knew there was no arguing with such a man. I knew what he wanted me to ask, but I would not give in to the temptation of Rebirth. That would have been against everything we stood for. It would have tarnished the legacy of the Guild and dishonoured all the dead. The appeal of Rebirth slithered further into my thoughts and I conceived of ways that Suchine could live anew, yet I could not bring myself to do it.

"He knew the risks," I said, sullen. "Swore the oaths. We all did."

"I can save him."

My eyes trembled as they met the Plague's. "You will not fool me. We do not fear death by your hand!"

"It is a simple question that I require you to answer," the Plague said. "Come and aid me and I shall grant you immortality for as long as you desire it." In my resolute silence, he sighed and unfurled a hand towards Suchine. "As a show of good faith, I shall not allow your poor friend to die." The chains holding Suchine upright pulsed and glowed a dark blue.

"What are you doing?" I shrieked.

Suchine stopped convulsing and his breathing deepened, though he remained unconscious. Relief flooded me, but it was short lived.

"Your answer," the Plague insisted. "What is it?"

The foundation of everything I once knew crumbled beneath me, and the only thing keeping me upright were his cold chains. I'd dedicated my long life to purging forbidden tech, and there I was before the worst Rebirth Doc of them all, forcing me to choose between the certain death of my comrades and myself, or succumbing to his vile ways.

Every word of his I still thought a lie, yet after he had healed Suchine, I started to wonder if he was not the outright villain I marked him as. "What happens if I refuse? You'll kill us all, right?"

The Plague scoffed. "I'm not as vulgar as you think I am. No, I will not kill you. I'll simply erase your memories and send you on your way. Though, I'm not sure how far you'll get without my help."

"And if I say yes?"

"I'll see to it that all of you get out of here alive," he said. "I'll still erase your memory of this encounter, but then I will restore it, at a time and place of my choosing, of course." His thumbs flicked in and out of his closed fists three more times. "Then you will abandon the oaths of this persecuting Guild and join me on my quest to kill Zenli and fortify the Velutra against the coming madness."

"What coming madness? What are you talking about?"

"Oh," he said with a cold smile. "You want answers? So do I."

I knelt there for a long moment, chained in silence. It didn't matter that all this had been for Zenli, I knew I was going to kill him for letting all my comrades die, for letting us fall into this trap. I would make sure he suffered the same anguish that burned inside every Guilder for their dead kin.

But I was hopeless at that moment. The promise I'd made on Bastion's name came back to me, as did my failure to protect Carellus, to protect Leonyd, Cosrick, and all who had died that day. I promised myself that I'd do everything in my power to get Rier and Suchine out of there alive and so I finally realised what I had to do.

I would have to become an aberration of the cosmos.

I would have to bide my time. It might not have been a month or a year from then, but I'd drive vengeance straight through his rotten heart. We'd killed Rebirth Docs before and they would just return in another body, in another place, and we'd have to start all over again. I knew there had to be a way to kill them once and for all, but the only way to do that would be to get close and learn his secrets. After all, that's why we had been ordered there in the first place. I still had a mission to complete.

"What do you say?" the Plague demanded. In that moment he seemed like a king of old, rivalling one of the Sages themselves. "Will you forsake your oaths to the Guild and swear new ones to me? Last chance, Ludaan."

Right there and then, I swallowed my past and forsook what I was. Everything I stood for. Holding my chin high, I looked up into the Plague's all-knowing eyes.

"I accept."

The Plague gave an approving nod, lips curled in that cunning smile. "In time you will come to understand, Ludaan, then you will think differently of me."

Before I could say or do anything else, everything went black.

CHAPTER THIRTEEN

A Velutran Farewell

Just like the Plague had said, the true memories came later.

What I did remember was that we made it down to the dungeon, but all we found was a dead man in chains with a leaking Rebirth signature. With Carellus dead, we could not check his mind for any discarded information, but judging by his melted eyes, his brain had been burnt to a crisp. Mission failure.

We escaped through the secret tunnel Carellus had discovered, unchallenged. Rier and I carried Suchine to the grav-sheath that rocketed us towards the other side of the moon's surface, where the waiting transport collected us. The soft thrumming of the engines provided some solace, as did the reserves that replenished our crystalas and immediately began healing our wounds, though Suchine remained unconscious and on the brink of death.

Once we were clear of the moon, we were about to ascend away and join the Mother Guild in a nearby star realm when scouts left behind amidst the dying battlefield pinged in my mind.

I connected to them just in time to watch immense black and spiked spheres tear into existence. Voidcrafts poured out; many of which were sword-shaped and stolen from Velutran owners, their elegance now defiled; others were created from their own cursed minds and had no purpose to their form except as an outlet of their madness. Drifting amongst them was a large network of thinly connected passageways—one of their travelling hive cities, as well as several asteroids carved into resplendent statues of Zenli, Her cursed self.

Yet greater than all the rest, larger than that dead moon, Zenli's personal voidcraft was a conglomerated mass of dead crafts and corpses, all shaped into an immense human face silently screaming against the stars.

"She's come," I murmured.

From its ruinous maw, a brewing darkness flashed out and struck the top of the fortress. A moment later, half the moon crunched in on itself to a singular point, and then was consumed in a perfect black sphere, distorting the remnants of the moon and icy rings all around it.

"What are you doing, Ludaan?" Rier cried. "Get us out of here!"

I spared the black heart one last look in my mind. There it would linger for billions of years as it feasted on the surrounding planets, slowly growing while it spewed out Malnetha's influence. I retreated from the feed and looked into Rier's desperate eyes right before we ascended away. "Costhrall protects us."

When I awoke aboard the Mother Guild, I couldn't remember much from our journey through the Cos Realm. My replenished crystala had barely kept me alive—my wounds were that severe—the same was true for Suchine and Rier. What I do recall from ascension was that my elan vital had teetered on the edge of joining the Cos Realm, but visions of Bastion had held me back. Perhaps because I had an unsettled score in his name.

Still in a haze, I laid there staring up at a starry ceiling, thinking about everything that had happened. How did it all go so wrong? The death of Bastion and the rest of my company stained my weary mind, carving out a hollow bitterness. The ache of my butchered arm was gone, but as I locked down at my regrown limb—the colour still pale compared to the rest of my dark skin—I wondered if I should have left it forever gone. As a reminder for all that was lost.

"You may have got your arm back, but we're not so easy to lose," a voice called out.

Groaning, I shifted to see Rier and Suchine sitting across the room, a dejected fatigue in their smiles. The only consolation out of that entire ordeal was that they were still alive. It was better than none of us coming back, though I would have traded places with any of the fallen.

"It seems Malnetha itself can't get rid of you if it tried," I muttered, unable to keep my lips from curling into a smile. "You don't know how much it warms my vital to see you both."

"Cos protects us, brother," Suchine said. He stood and walked over, as did Rier, though she came around to the other side of my bed, and both were draped in the pale green robes of mourning that had also been wreathed around me. "Alas, too many have returned to its fold."

My head fell, solemn. "Too many."

"We failed," Suchine said, bowing his head in defeat. "Even the sluugrall Rier collected was destroyed on our escape."

"It's probably for the best," Rier said with a sigh. "Malnetha stoked my greed down there. I should have destroyed it without hesitation. If it had fallen into the wrong hands…"

"At least it's over for now," Suchine said. "We can—"

"It is never over," Rier interrupted, clenching a fist in the air. "The Guild will regroup and return stronger than ever. We will embark on a crusade of terrible retribution against the Zenlians and show them no quarter."

"We will never forget the fallen," I said, eagerly nodding, but then the faces of the dead burned behind my eyes, weakening my resolve. Cosrick. Leonyd. Carellus. Bastion. I snuffed the grief down and glanced past Rier out the small window, the stars faint in their silent singing. "Where are we now?"

"Zenli's fleet only stayed to watch the moon die, then they left," Rier said. "So, the Guild Mother moved us back to this realm's star. Decided it was worth the risk of being attacked again to give all the fallen a true Velutran farewell to the star closest where they died."

Suchine scratched at his black beard. "We're all waiting for you. Come on, you're no good to anyone lying down." He paused, then placed a sombre hand on my shoulder. "Commander."

The word stung to hear, though I knew Bastion was proud of me. I swore to myself that I would give my everything to lead the Guild's swords with as much resolve, strength, and compassion as he did.

I swung off the side of the bed and for the first time since I had left the safety of the Mother Guild's foundation, I felt I could be at ease once more.

We didn't say a word to one another as we walked throughout the quiet corridors. When we reached the hangar, nearly every Guilder was gathered there, a sea of hazy green against the pure white hall. Cospriests walked amongst them just as they had for our descension, misty rivers flowing upwards, though now I certainly didn't care for their benedictions. They'd done us no good on the mission.

Floating before the ranks of soldiers was a large gathering of white coffins. The bodies that had been recovered were cleaned, and those who had been obliterated with the moon or devoured before now had a single green flower placed inside in remembrance. All the coffins faced the immense window where the craft's hull had retracted for the ceremony.

The dark void was nowhere to be seen. In its place, the Mother Star of this realm loomed in its cosmic immensity; a swollen sphere of white and yellow light, yearning to destroy us if it weren't for the craft's shields, blinding if it weren't for the crystalas protecting our eyes. The star was covered in what looked like bubbling grains of sand—each the size of the moon we'd just fought on—all rising and falling, hypnotic. Several dark patches like rotting wounds marred its otherwise brilliant magnificence.

I found my place in the hangar, right at the very front alongside Suchine and Rier. They both shed sullen tears, as did most of those gathered, yet my eyes remained dry from the shock. The hardened swords of the Guild never wept, but when the blade itself cracked, what else could be done?

Sage Tienza was present, beside whom stood the Guild Mother, both reduced to the same emerald robes as their subjects. Although no words were spoken between us, the guilt that mired their weary eyes said everything.

I do not blame them or myself for what happened. Blame is a thing that can be passed from hand to hand all the way back to Malnetha and Costhrall in their creation of the cosmos. Blame is a useless thing and I have always strived to scour it from my mind whenever it tries to take root.

I looked over the coffins, and although they were all unmarked—for in death we were all equal—I could detect that Bastion's coffin was right before me. I pictured him lying peacefully inside, the same man I had met in that grim city all those years ago. The man who had lifted me up from the filth and raised me as his son.

My father now forever gone.

As the coffins hurtled out towards that blazing star on their final journey to the Cos Realm, the weight of grief fell on me heavier than ever before.

CHAPTER FOURTEEN

My Oath

I never intended to taste immortality. But I did.

The Plague found me a year later spying on a known hideout of Zenlian sympathisers. He came in the form of an old beggar on those dusty streets of a forsaken planet, begging for some serum, but when he flicked his thumbs out of his closed fist three times, I was struck dumb as memories flooded back to my mind.

When the rush settled, I looked into the eyes of that old man and saw the Plague as he was in the depths of that dead moon's heart. I formed a blade and lunged at him, but just as Bastion had grasped me as a defenceless child, I froze as his crystala strangled me. A thin smile cracked around his dry lips.

"You swore an oath to me, Ludaan," he said, his voice a dagger of ice in my mind.

That I had.

I have left this, the first of my mortal memories, drifting in the black gulf as a capsule for those who may come after. To show them what once was; why I fought. Regardless if I fail or succeed in my task, I hope that if my story is found that it stirs something within. That whoever is bold enough to relive the horrors as I did shall learn from our mistakes and continue the eternal fight against Malnetha. Even now as I sit upon the brink of oblivion, reflecting on my long life, the Great Darkness tightens its stranglehold on our galaxy. It does not rest.

Nor shall I.

Reviews

Dear reader, you have my sincerest gratitude for giving your time to read this story. If I can ask only one more thing, it is that you leave an honest review on Amazon or Goodreads. Reviews are the best way to support indie authors so we can shine, but more importantly, so our stories can find their way into the minds of other readers such as yourself. These tales we write only live on in your memories, and by sharing your experience, they will endure. Thank you for your support, it means the world, I mean entire galaxy.

About the Author

Born and raised in Australia, Calum Lott is the science-fantasy author of a Dirge For Cascius, Arkoma, and the series My Mortal Memories, all set in the vast Valsollas galaxy. His greatest inspirations are the video game Bloodborne, the manga Berserk and The Lord of the Rings. In his spare time, you'll find Calum adequately playing the guitar, reading at a snail's pace, watching movies (LOTR over and over), annoying his gorgeous partner or sitting at his laptop writing stories whilst getting a sore arse.